BEFORE

I

DIED!

Jules Mitchell

1

ISBN: 9781520726939

2

To Sarah & Colin
Best friends for
Life
Love You
Jules xxxx

To my wonderful Husband John

Thank you for all your help and support

3

Prologue

I feel like I'm floating, yes I am floating, up down, twisting like a kite. I am feeling like a feather, yes that's it, a beautiful white feather dancing in the breeze, I feel happy, content. More content than I have ever felt before, a strange feeling like I haven't a care in the whole wide world, arrrh floating, floating I feel free, I feel wonderful, I feel....what is that noise that has broken into my beautiful silent world, a loud noise, a harsh noise. I can't quite fathom what it is but it's getting louder and louder. I still have no idea but still it gets louder, louder, louder....it's screaming, I can hear screaming, I can hear so much screaming and shouting, I can hear people shouting then more screaming more screaming more screaming !!!!!

I am dead, I realise that now, and the screaming I heard was all the other people dying around me as the plane plummeted in to the ocean. I don't know quite how I feel other than very very sad. Sad that I will miss all the things I was hoping for in my new life. Arrrh my new life, I have waited for a long long time to get my new life and now it was ready to collect me I will miss it. The train that was to take me to my future has just left the station without me....no more looking forward, no more plans.

I am dead !

Chapter ONE

The sun is shining through my office window; it is such a wonderful spring day. The trees are laden with blossom and the smell in the air on my way to work this morning was wonderful. I ordered my bagel from the receptionist on the first floor as I came in and the little teenage delivery boy with the ginger hair and freckles has just dropped it on my desk.

Things are good in the world today, I am meeting Simon straight from work, we are going to see the early showing of the new James Bond movie and then off for dinner at my favourite restaurant, Ruby in the Dust. This Friday night is going to be great. I have known Simon for five whole weeks now and we have been out on eight or nine occasions. Each time has been great - I think I might even be falling for him although all my friends say "give it a bit longer before you wear your heart on your sleeve - he has got a bit of a reputation for not being great serious boyfriend material". Of course I know best and I think he is wonderful.

I am just finishing off for the day when my boss Mr Clever (I always think that is a great name for a man who is actually very clever - but he always pronounces it Cleever), asks me if I have a few minutes just to do a short email for him to a client who is desperate to review it over the weekend. "Short email" I am thinking - when he needs the week end to review it? Well, about five pages of typing later, I realise I am the sole person left in the office and it is half past six. I was supposed to be outside the cinema at five forty-five, I expect Simon will have tried to call me but I always shut my mobile off when I am in the office. Still I am sure he will understand - he knows my job is important to me. I tidy my desk, switch off my computer and grab my jacket, shouting a quick goodbye to the man sitting on the security desk at the bottom of the stairs, I rush out to the cinema.

When I get to the Rex there is no sign of Simon anywhere. I switch on my mobile and there are three missed calls. Relief washes over me. He called, arhh how sweet I thought. But none of them was from Simon, just two from my mum with the one message asking if I was going to Asda tomorrow and if so would I get her a bottle of Prosecco and then one from my friend Mary who left her usual message of "hi gal, oh - not there so will call again soon love ya!". I stood for a moment or two then thought "Well stuff you Simon, I'll go in on my own".

The movie was only a few minutes in when I got to my seat - they had probably been showing the usual twenty adverts beforehand. I settled in the seat and took a sip from my diet coke, just a small one, although that was almost as big as my head. The movie was OK but not as good as I was expecting but hey, I can at least say I've seen it now.

I strolled out of the Rex wondering just what to do next when a hand suddenly grabbed my shoulder, spinning me around to come face to face with a very angry looking Simon. The shock of my expression must have jolted something in his head as he suddenly dropped the fierceness in his eyes and his face immediately softened.

"I was so worried about you" he said "when you didn't show up I thought you might have had an accident, I know you wouldn't just let me down for nothing". Let me down, a strange term I thought at the time but it went straight over my head as he squeezed me tight and kissed my ear.

I explained all about the last minute work I had been asked to do and that as my job was important to me I was happy to oblige my boss and that as I never keep my phone on in the office I didn't get his call. Then I thought but he didn't call! Still never mind. Simon was saying that my boss takes me for granted and that I should claim overtime if he ever asks me to stay late again. I explained that in the position I am at work, a little extra time is part and parcel of my contract. I do not claim overtime as such, I get a review once a year and a bonus which more than covers any extra time and effort I put into my job, and anyway I love my job and am happy to do it. I thought I saw a sulky expression appear but it was soon replaced with another hug and "Right let's go eat I'm starving". All thoughts of irritation at his remarks were lost as we both bounced off to the Ruby in the Dust for a lovely dinner.

Time went by and within six weeks I decided I was head over heels in love with this man. OK he had a few faults but who hasn't? Like the time my car broke down so I was late to meet him and he accused me of flirting with the breakdown man although he'd never even seen the breakdown man. Then there was the occasion of my mother's birthday lunch which was just for the family members. When I got to his house after the lunch was over he was in a foul mood, saying he couldn't understand why he wasn't invited- and just who was there other than family? I had to show him my pictures on my phone to convince him that it was in fact just us and no other man was with me.

I put all this jealousy down to insecurity. I had heard rumours from my friends that he had been madly in love with a girl in the past who had cheated on him a lot and he was very suspicious of it happening again if he let his guard down. That's how he got a reputation of being a flirt, a "love 'em and leave 'em" type of bloke, he was determined not to let himself fall in love again. Give him time I thought, that's all he needs, lots of love and lots of time. I can convince him that I am not the type who would cheat on him.

My mum thought he was nice but a little strange, and told me to be careful. I wasn't quite sure just what she meant but as I was falling for him by the time she told me that, I chose to ignore her remarks.

Another six weeks went by and everything was wonderful. Simon was attentive, kind, courteous, generous and hadn't shown any more signs of jealousy or anger so I convinced myself that he was feeling more confident about our relationship and was beginning to trust again. I knew he loved me, as he told me lots of times, especially when we made love but then a lot of men say that when aroused and having sex.

I really believed him though and even more so when we were sitting having dinner in our local Indian restaurant and he produced a "friendship" ring as he called it. It wasn't an actual engagement ring he said, just an "I love you Tilly, so maybe we should move in together" ring. The waiter saw my delight and brought us over a glass of bubbly each to celebrate. I think I was so shocked and happy that I had no problem in saying "yes, of course we should!". We sat for the rest of the evening making plans. Yes, it was better if he moved in with me rather than us move into his flat as mine was much more central to everything. Even though it was a little smaller than his it was nicer in a lot of other ways. I had no doubt this was the start of a wonderful future and was so excited to hear about all he planned for us to do in the days, weeks and years to come.

My mother was sort of happy for me, she said she hoped everything would work out well but when I prompted her for the obvious doubts she had about Simon she just shrugged and said that she just wanted what was best for me and that if I was happy that was all that mattered. I have since learned that mother's intuitions are not to be sniffed at. I wish I had pushed her for more explanation of her doubts, but I was so happy I really didn't give too much thought to her hesitation. Maybe it was just a mother's protective shield that put doubts in her head. She wouldn't want to upset me if there was no real reason, so kept them locked inside.

Moving day arrived. I had taken three days off work and so had Simon so we could get his stuff in and get settled. I had planned a really nice dinner to cook for the first night with a bottle of wine chilling in the fridge ready. Excitement was not the word for it, it was elation. I was walking on air as I went to get milk, bread and other bits for our first breakfast the next day. Simon was due to arrive with his borrowed van full of his belongings at 10.00am. Mr Patel's shop was only about a five minute walk from my flat so I floated off at about 9.40am. Haneen Patel, Mr Patel's wife, (funny I call him Mr Patel but call her Haneen), anyway she was in the shop that morning and was always up for a chat and I was more than happy to oblige - after all it was a special day for me, the man I love was moving in with me, I would at last have somebody to go home to, cook special meals for (although not all, I would expect Simon to share in things) Having never lived with anyone other than my parents before it all seemed so exciting and I just wanted to share this excitement with anyone who would listen. Before I realised it , it was ten past ten, "oh I had better be off" I told

Haneen, I had my man to see to. We both laughed and off I went, actually I think I may even have skipped.

His face said it all when I walked through the door...the anger. Well not so much anger but actual rage, I even thought I could see steam coming out of his ears at one stage.

"Whatever is up", I said, thinking something must have gone terribly wrong with the flat.

"You" he growled, "You, that's what is wrong, you! You were supposed to be here at ten - where the bloody hell were you? I thought you must have changed your mind and weren't going to show up!" But suddenly the anger subsided and I could see tears start to glisten in the corners of his eyes "I.,.I ,oh I am so sorry" he tried to stretch his arms out to me but I backed away, I didn't know what to think, how could he think I would go to all this trouble of getting him to move his stuff into the flat if I wasn't going to actually let him move in...I softened as the memory of what my friends had said about his previous girlfriend letting him down so badly flashed through my mind. Slowly I put my arms out to him and he grabbed at me as if he hadn't seen me in

14

weeks. Sobbing into my shoulder he said he was sorry again and again for doubting our relationship. Again and again I comforted him and said I would never leave him, although small doubts were beginning to creep into my head about his actual sincerity - and maybe even his sanity. Once I had explained all about going to the corner shop and having a giggle with Haseen and just how excited I had been about getting provisions for his breakfast he seemed to relax. I, on the other hand, began to feel like I was consoling a frightened child but dismissed the thought quickly when he started to kiss me and then lift and carry me over to the bedroom.

Although we had made love to each other loads of times, as it was now in "our" flat and not just mine it felt it should be sort of extra special. Well it was, but I must admit although it was exciting it was a little rough at times. I just put it down to the thrill of being together for the first time as an officially living together couple. As we lay in each other's arms after, all the thoughts of before and worries about his strange behaviour were totally erased from my mind, I was feeling so very happy.

15

"Did you say you had food "? Simon suddenly jumped out of bed and pulled me up behind him and giving me a gentle tap on my bottom shooed me into the kitchen to get some food ready. "Makes you hungry all this loving eh?" He shouted from the shower "don't be too long I'm ravenous". "Hey" I shouted back "you can cook too remember, I'm not your slave" I shouted back and then added "how do you like you eggs anyway?" but almost before I could finish the sentence he was behind me and had hold of my hair, pulling me backwards.

"What did you mean by that remark?" he screamed at me. "What, about your eggs?" I said, thinking this was some kind of joke he was acting out, but he started pulling harder on my hair. "Ouch!" I said. "Simon you're hurting me, enough now!" but he just kept pulling,

"No, the remark about you not being my slave" he said. "Why did you say that, you bitch?". I started to slide down lower and lower as he was pulling at my hair and began to cry out in pain.

"I didn't mean anything by it, it was just a joke! Get off Simon, you are really frightening me now!" I must have screamed this as he suddenly let go and pulled me to him. "I'm so sorry" he said yet again. "I don't know what came over me, please forgive me. I promise it will never happen again!

Although I didn't know it at the time, that was a statement I was going to get very, very, used to hearing.

Chapter TWO

For the next three or four weeks things were fantastic, Simon was the perfect gent, helping with the housework, well occasionally making the bed really, but he did come shopping with me sometimes - and even once he actually cooked me beans on toast. He never washed up though, or even offered to, just ate his meals and then went and sat on the sofa with the TV remote or sometimes a newspaper, never a book. He never stayed in the little kitchen and chatted while I washed up and tidied away. I didn't really worry about this at the beginning though, as it was quite nice playing at house for my man. There was a tiny breakfast bar in the kitchen and it would have been lovely though if he would just sit there and chat. I did suggest this to him once but he just said a woman's role in the house is doing the chores and he should try and stay out of the way while I was busy doing just that. I took this as one of his strange humorous statements, but I know differently now.

I don't really know exactly when I started to get an uneasy feeling about our relationship. It sort of crept up on me very slowly. Maybe the seed was initially sown into my mind the day we went to visit my mother. She had invited us over for Sunday lunch, which I was really looking forward to as I hadn't seen her for some weeks. Well it all started off innocently enough. Simon hadn't been that keen to go - making all kinds of excuses - but in the end as he could see I wasn't going to back down he decided to agree.

We both got ready, I had bought a new dress a few days before and decided I would wear it and show my mum that I didn't always dress in jeans and t-shirts. I was admiring myself in the mirror in the bedroom when Simon sneaked up behind me and grabbing me around the waist planted a big kiss on the back of my neck, I must admit I was quite pleased as I thought it was going to lead into him saying how nice my new dress looked and how he was beginning to look forward to going out with me...but as I turned to put my arms around him in response to his affection he grabbed my shoulders really quite hard and his face suddenly turned to that hideous expression I had learned to recognise as his "you are mine and don't forget it" expression.

"Whatever is wrong?" I asked him, quite innocently really, as I couldn't think of anything that could make him cross.

"You don't see it do you Matilda?" He always used that name when he was cross with me about something, although my actual name is just Tilly!

"I have no idea what you are talking about" I answered, but I could feel his grip on my shoulders tightening as I spoke.

"You!" he started to scream at me."You! We are only going to your fucking mother's for god's sake, not some fucking society wedding! Take that ridiculous dress off and put your jeans back on, you look disgusting. Just who are you expecting to see at your mothers today then? Has she got a new man lined up for you eh? I know she doesn't like me. Well, just what is it that would make you dress up so beautifully?"

His squeeze on my arms was making me feel a little queasy so I shouted back at him to let me go but that only heightened his anger, then, as soon as it started it finished, with the usual rubbish – "Sorry", cuddle, kiss, "Don't know why I do it, I love you so much" and then, as usual, I forgave him and ended up cuddling him while he sobbed. Then I changed into my jeans and off we went to my mothers. Why I didn't do something then I shall never know.

After this episode I decided it must be me. I am giving off some sort of air that I am going to be unfaithful or leave him or, well I don't know what - but it must be me. After all, he has given up his flat to move in with me and has stopped seeing his friends. Well I only knew of one real friend he had but he doesn't speak of him any more so I suppose they no longer see each other. We are happy, yes. Yes of course we are, I tell myself, we are really happy. When he has these outbursts it is only when he feels insecure and that is probably because I make him feel that way. Yes I must make an effort to reassure him that I am happy, we are happy. There is no need for him to even think for one moment that I would rather be with somebody else.

21

I formed a plan a couple of days later, I would do some reassuring by making him a surprise dinner of his favourite food and favourite wine and I'd dress in something special. I would put the little fold up table out in the lounge and lay it with a tablecloth and some candles. It would be a really lovely surprise for when he got home from work. I had taken a half day off work and gone to the supermarket and bought all the necessities for our special night and had actually spent almost a whole month's food budget, but I thought it worth is as I would give him a night to remember (which it did in fact turn out to be, but for different reasons!) Well the dinner was all but ready to serve. I was dressed in the dress he loved to see me in most (I wonder why I put on his favourite dress instead of the one I liked best!). I heard his key in the door and, smiling, I went into the lounge armed with the bottle opener ready to surprise him.

"What the fuck is going on here then" he said on entering the flat "expecting company then were you?" The look on his face said it all.

"W-w-hat," I stammered expecting him to do the exact opposite of what he did "I-I-I, thought I would surprise you with a special evening, I've got your favourite dinner ready, I-I-I thought you would be pleased"...My head hit the floor with a terrible thud and for a moment I blacked out completely. When I came to I focused on the face of the devil, I swear, his was so red and so angry and his fist was raised. I wondered if I was dead or would be very soon. "Stop it!" I yelled but his fist made contact with my temple as I dodged to one side to try and avoid the punch "Stop it for god's sake! What is wrong with you?" I screamed again. Once again the blow hit my temple and this time I blacked out completely.

When I came to I was in my bed, Simon was sitting next to me with a bowl of warm water, a flannel and a towel, tears were streaming down his face and a huge sob emitted from his body.

"Oh my darling, what have I done to you, I am so sorry, please forgive me please" another huge sob and his arms were suddenly around me and he was stroking my hair and whispering "Forgive me Tilly, please forgive me".

I was a little too stunned, shocked and probably concussed but also awake enough to be very frightened so I snuggled up to him and let him sob. All I could think of was why oh why, then as if by magic a thought crept slowly into my addled brain....it's not me...stupid....it HIM !!!!!!!!!!!

How I actually made it through the night, snuggled up next to the devil I do not know but something in me said "leave it for now while he is rational, wait it out, tomorrow, yes tomorrow you can do something about it".

Unbelievably, the next morning there he was, in the kitchen making me toast and coffee of all things. Not a mention of the night before, and making me breakfast...well that was so unlike him.

"What do I do?" I thought, "Challenge him or what?"

I had no need to worry, he sat me down at the little breakfast bar, grabbed my hands and moved me so I was opposite him, pushed my coffee and toast in front of me. I was thinking so here it is, the apology, here is the 'I am so sorry,' here is the 'it will never happen again', here is the 'I love you so very much'.

Slowly I was beginning to think well maybe this time he will actually mean it but then he leaned almost nose to nose with me, gripped my hands and said very slowly, not "I am sorry", not "This will never happen again", not "I love you so very much", but "Mess me about and I will kill you!" and with that he punched me straight in the face, stood up and said in a really nasty voice "You had better be here when I get home or I will find you and kill you" and with that he walked calmly out of the flat and was gone.

I don't know exactly how long I sat at that little breakfast bar, I know there was a trickle of blood that had run from my nose and that it had dried hard on my cheek, I know that my head was fuzzy, I know that I was finding it harder and harder to breath, not because of his attack on me physically but because I was getting more and more hysterical inside. I had read somewhere that if you have a panic attack you should grab a paper bag and breath into it...I glanced around the tiny kitchen but could see no obvious sign of any paper bags, well only a plastic carrier bag with the name of my friend Haneen's corner shop printed on the side "Patel's

Shop around the corner – Always open" which was not quite true but almost. I decided plastic was not quite the thing for a panic attack, the thought of this actually made me smile and suddenly I wasn't finding it quite so difficult to breath.

I looked up to check the time on my pretty little chicken clock, the one I had bought with some birthday money I had got from my grandmother about four years ago. I had wanted to buy something that would always remind me of her and thought what better than a clock, after all I look at the clock several times every day so would obviously think of her often and luckily she is still alive, although now cared for in a nursing home, and healthy even in her 90th year. I stood up slowly and a little unsteadily, holding on to the work top and walked over to the tiny mirror I had sitting on the windowsill next to a slightly dried up pot with a single geranium. I dared to look at the sight that was going to look back at me. Thankfully my nose was not broken as I had first dreaded it would be, but there was quite a lot of blood on my face. He must have had a catch nail or something (at lease I hope it was a finger nail and not something worse) as

I had a huge gash just under my eye. The blood from that had mingled with the stuff that had come from my nose and my cheeks and nose were beginning to puff up quite badly, I looked for all the world like I had gone three rounds with Mike Tyson and not come off well. I reached up to the cupboard and pulled out a cereal bowl, filled it with lukewarm water and a little salt (my grandmother's answer to anything medical...bathe it in salt water darling, that will kill the germs and make it heal quicker) I don't know if there is an ounce of truth in this statement but as I had just looked at my chicken clock and thought of her I felt slightly comforted to do as she would have done. Very gently I bathed my face using a clean jay cloth I had by the sink, too unsteady to go to the bathroom for cotton wool.

It was 11.15am, I had sat in that kitchen for over three hours, well that meant it was three hours since the "devil" as I now called him in my head, had left me there literally a bleeding wreck. Now anger started to well up inside me, totally overtaking the shock I had felt previously, my face hurt, even more with the stinging of salty water, but my anger was reaching a crescendo, it was overtaking any fear, hurt or pain I had felt earlier.

Anger is a strange thing. It can make you strong, very strong and the more I got angry the more I thought "How dare he do this to me, how dare he threaten me?" All the little niggles I had been feeling for the past few weeks, and even before that. The little niggles that I had pushed to one side thinking at first that is was my imagination and later that it must be of my own making, to get him jealous or angry by what I said or even what I was wearing. So angry in fact that I thought I am going to be here when he comes back. I am not going to run as I had first thought I would, I am going to stand up to him, after all, it is my flat, he can just bugger off. I'll never succumb to his violence again – "If he comes near me I will be ready" I thought, as I took my heavy wooden rolling pin out of the kitchen drawer and placed it on the worktop. The thought of the rolling pin in my hand raised up ready to smash him over the head made me smile. Well it started to until the pain of smiling jolted me back to reality.

After I cleaned myself up I switched on the coffee machine, put in a capsule of espresso and picked a mug out of the cupboard, my favourite mug with a picture of Niagara Falls on the side, a place I always vowed to myself I would visit someday. The mug that the devil always used for himself as he liked it, he often said he would take me there one day, well that was in his loving moments anyway. I pressed the machine into action and sat back against the breakfast bar cradling my mug between my hands.

A plan I thought, I must devise a plan. I knew he wouldn't be home for hours yet so I switched on my laptop and headed the new file..."Getting rid of the DEVIL". Before I could formulate my plan though, I would need to list all the things that had happened to make me want to say goodbye to Simon forever. I know after last night and this morning I shouldn't need to even think about why, but deep down inside me I worried that I still had feelings that I couldn't completely kill. That sounds ridiculous but emotions are strange things. I wanted him to go, I needed him to go. I wanted to feel safe and I wasn't sure I felt safe with him the way he was. I know maybe I was to blame in some instances but maybe I should have helped him get over his problems, maybe persuaded him to go to a counsellor, even gone with him.

An hour passed and I had still not devised my plan. I had listed all the awful things he had done to me mentally and physically and I had constructed a 'for and against' list. The 'against' list was at least three times as long as the 'for' though, but despite that I had almost talked myself out of it when I heard the front door open. I glanced up at the chicken clock and it only said it was 1.45pm, my stomach suddenly started to churn, my face was beginning to hurt again as the aspirin I had swallowed with my coffee was starting to wear off. I pushed myself up from the stool, closed my laptop and started to reach for the rolling pin. I have no idea just what I intended to do, or in fact what to expect, for goodness sake I had just been talking myself out of even asking him to leave, why was I so nervous now....the front door closed and the kitchen door opened, I tightened my grip on the rolling pin and stared and waited. The first thing I saw was a hand holding a huge bunch of flowers appearing around the side of the door, followed by a second hand holding a bottle of prosecco, then he appeared, a great sheepish grin on his face. There we both stood, looking at each other like idiots. I wasn't sure whether to smile, although that would hurt, or to rant or to actually go up to him and hug him. I have wondered on many occasions since just what would have happened if I had done anything other than what I actually did.

"Oh my god" Simon said when he had had time to register what my face looked like and putting the flowers and wine down on to the breakfast bar he came towards me, "whatever happened to you my darling?"

I crumbled, all the hate disappeared, feelings that I thought were gone came rushing back, my fear of him completely gone. I let him hold me, I let him comfort me, I let him be my man yet again.

Chapter THREE

After we had settled with a meal on our laps, which of course I had cooked, I started to explain what he had done and how frightened I had been. He cried, said he was so very sorry but this time I did make a stand and say he must get some help which to my surprise he readily agreed to. Anything, he said, anything to keep it from happening again, he apparently didn't remember anything about the outbursts, either last night or this morning and certainly didn't remember telling me he would kill me. We went to bed and he was so gentle and kind, we made beautiful love with him being careful not to hurt my face.

When I woke up the next morning he was gone. I must have been really tired as I usually woke up as soon as he moved out of the bed. Never mind, I thought, today is the start of our new life together. I was so optimistic, I really believed him when he said he was going to go to his GP today to get referred to somebody for some professional help. Luckily for me I had a few days owing for me to take off so I called into work and told them I would finish the couple of emails I had to do at home on my laptop and then take the few days I had owing off. That would save having to explain just why I looked like a failed boxing champion.

I ran myself a nice bath filled with my favourite bath oils and was feeling quite light hearted as I finished my emails and went to get my bath. Relaxing into the beautiful soft fragrant water I closed my eyes, I must have drifted into a shallow sleep because I didn't hear the front door open, or the kitchen door or the bathroom door but suddenly I opened my eyes to see the Devil staring down on me, my laptop held above his head.

"Think you could get rid of me did you? " his voice didn't sound human, his face was more terrifying than I had ever seen it look before. I had no time to grab my protective rolling pin as that was still in the kitchen.

"What is wrong Simon?", I tried to reason with him in a calm voice but before I could get the whole sentence out my laptop came crashing down on me.

"I read it Matilda, I read it! I read your list!" as I tried to scramble out of the bath he was raining punches down on me, trying to push me under the water. I managed to reach up enough to protect my face at the same time desperately grabbing uselessly at the plug to try and let the water out.

"You will never get rid of me you fucking stupid bitch" he growled "I knew exactly what I did to you the other night. I'm a good actor aren't I? Did you think for one minute that I wasn't aware of my actions? You are even more stupid than I thought, of course I know what I am doing, don't worry I am not going to kill you today, but I will one day and you won't be able to stop me. Now get out of this bloody bath, get yourself dressed and make me some dinner. As from now you are my slave and you'll never get away, you hear me? Never!"

And with that last statement he pushed me hard in the face and stormed out of the bathroom. I was shivering uncontrollably by this time, due not only to the cold bath water, but the shock and pain of the past thirty minutes. I really thought he was going to kill me. My laptop was lying open on the bottom of the bath where he had tried to hit me on the head with it but I had just managed to duck so it crashed straight into the water. It was obvious that is would never work again. He must have come straight in and read my list, he must have actually searched my files for it, as when I had finished my emails for work, (oh how I wish I had shut it all down) I must have left it unprotected and he must have seen the file marked "escape the Devil".

I wrapped myself in my bath robe tying the belt as tightly as I could around my waist just in case Simon saw me as I ran from the bathroom to the bedroom to get some clothes. All I could think of was that I had to get out of the flat, I had to escape whatever horrors were waiting for me. There was no sign of him as I crept into the bedroom - he must have been in the kitchen because to get to the bedroom I had to walk through the lounge. The kitchen door was closed. Huh, I thought to myself, all the times I wished he would stay in the kitchen with me and all he would do was loaf in the lounge and now he is in there.

Then I thought but what the bloody hell is he doing in there? I quickly got dressed in my jeans and a sweater, dried my hair on a towel that luckily was lying over the radiator - I didn't want to go back out to the bathroom to get one as I thought he might be out there now. I needed my bag though. It had my car keys in it, and my purse and everything. "Shit, I thought, that means I have to get into the kitchen to retrieve them and that means the Devil will be there."

I looked around the bedroom for something heavy I could take as protection. I settled on a squash racket - I know that sounds stupid but I thought at least I might be able to push it in his face or something, although I had no real idea and there was nothing else I thought I could do any kind of damage with. Slowly I opened the bedroom door and peeped out, no sign, I crept into the lounge and still no sign. Slowly, very slowly and shaking like a leaf I opened the kitchen door just a crack.

Simon was sitting at the breakfast bar with the same evil expression on his face. "Come on in Matilda" he growled "I have been waiting for you...what delights are you going to cook for me tonight my little slave?" and he began to laugh, a gruesome throaty unbelievably horrendous laugh. My eyes searched the kitchen in record time looking for where I had placed my bag. I spotted it on the window sill next to the mirror I had been using to survey my injured face only the day before. He must have noticed my eye scanning the room because before I had time to move a muscle he jumped up and grabbed my bag and held it out in front of him.

"Is this what you wanted my little slave?" His sickening voice made me want to throw up. "Come now, you didn't think I was going to let you out of the flat, did you?"

He moved towards me but just as he was about to grab me I realised the rolling pin was still on the side, and within my grasp. I had no time to think of anything but grabbing the wooden weapon and swinging it at his head. The first attempt missed completely and I almost threw myself with it but as he reached out to defend himself he knocked me backwards which gave me more balance to lunge forward again and this time I didn't miss.

Crack! I got him right on his temple. His face screwed up as he felt the impact and as he lifted his hand to feel for the damage he let go of my bag. My second swing really caught him off balance and he went down on one knee, which just gave me enough time to grab my bag and head for the door. I was just about to dive through it when he grabbed my ankle and started to pull me backwards.

The next few seconds were like something out of a movie. I can only assume it was something to do with the vibration in the kitchen, although I would rather think it was my grandmothers intervention, but my chicken clock fell off the wall, and although not that heavy it was just heavy enough to only hurt a little but definitely to shock him when it landed on top of his head. For a nanosecond he loosened his grip on my leg and I pulled myself free.

I slammed the door hard, hopefully shutting it hard on his hand, I didn't wait to find out as I was out of the flat, down the stairs in seconds and didn't glance back, as I was convinced if I did so my face would be met with a fist or worse. I ran to my car, unlocking it with the remote as I ran, it was only parked about fifty metres away but it felt like miles, then to my horror I realised my car was blocked in.

My heart began to sink and I looked around me frantically for an alternative escape route. I knew that if I ran he would be able to catch me easily, he was far fitter than me which he had proved to me on many occasions when we were at the gym together, where I would be exhausted after three miles on the treadmill. Simon could go on for ten without even puffing.

Still not daring to look behind me, my guardian angel (or maybe my grandmothers instinct) suddenly appeared in the shape of my next door neighbour, just pulling away in her obviously not blocked in car. I shouted to Emma and was relieved to see her turn instantly and beckon to me to get in.

"Wow I am glad to see you" I panted, as she edged her way from the curb. As we slowly moved away I just caught sight of "the Devil" arriving at my stationary car and, realising it was empty, searching up and down the street with those poisonous eyes. It was only when we were at the end of the road that I managed to calm down a little, my heart was still racing but my shaking was beginning to subside.

"Where to" Emma was asking. "I'm off to Asda - do you want to come with me? When I saw you car was blocked in

I was just going to knock and ask if you wanted to come with me, but then I thought I saw Simon's car there so thought if Simon was at home too you probably had some better plans." It was only when we got to the traffic lights that Emma eventually turned to face me.

"My god Tilly, have you had an accident?"

The returning look on my face said everything Emma wanted to know.

"I'm taking you straight to the police station, he's got to be locked up if he did that to you, it was Simon wasn't it?" Suddenly my tears were uncontrollable, and my sobs could probably be heard in Scotland.

Emma parked outside the police station and turned to me "Ready?" she said, unlocking her seat belt. I didn't move, just stared at the movement going on in front of me. Cars reversing, people coming and going, one police car moved in front of us and turned on it's siren before pulling out into the traffic.

I swung around to look at Emma, "I can't do it " I said "He needs help in some sort of hospital not locked up in a police cell.

"Now look here" Emma scolded me gently "just look in the mirror Tilly" she adjusted her rear view mirror so I could see the state of myself. "If you don't get this sorted now he will probably go on to do it to the next person to fall for him. Look," she softened even more, "I know you thought you loved him and you owe him something but for heaven's sake he could have killed you, in fact he might even try again. You need him completely out of your life forever." she put her hand on mine and gently squeezed it. "Come on" she said softly, "I'll be beside you all the time".

Slowly I undid my seatbelt and opened the door but just as I was about to get out I saw Simon's car come sweeping into the car park in front of us. I froze for a second and Emma noticing my stiffness and followed my gaze

"That's his car!" she blurted. "What the hell is he doing?"

We both stared at Simon who didn't give us a second look, well he probably wouldn't have recognised Emma's car anyway with all the other similar versions of Renault Cleos in the car park, surely he wasn't going to give himself up? I clipped my seat belt back on as quickly as possible.

"Please take me to my mum's Emma, please."

She didn't argue, just clipped herself in and turned the key in the ignition.

Thankfully I could see my mother was in when we arrived as her car was in the drive, I just hoped that she would be on her own and didn't have a house full of old cronies doing cross stitch as she tended to do. Emma refused my invitation to come in with me for a coffee explaining she had to get to Asda, but really I thought she had probably had enough of me for one day anyway. She waved goodbye and blew me a kiss, and mouthed the words "You know where I am if you need me", and was gone.

My mother had been standing at the door step since we pulled up and looked very worried.

"What an earth happened to you?" were her first words as I walked up the front path towards her. "Has there been an accident? Is Simon alright? Was it in the car?"

All these questions made my head spin although I knew they would have to be answered - but not at this very moment.

I walked into the kitchen, pulled out one of the chairs and flopped onto it with my poor anxious mother two feet behind me. She knew better than to push me so she busied herself filling the kettle and spooning coffee into the cafetiere. On her third spoonful I put my hand over hers and said, "I think that's enough now mum" and with that burst into tears. She cradled me in her arms and for the first time in days I felt safe.

We held each other for quite some time, beautiful memories of my childhood came flooding back, how if I fell off my bike or lost a favourite toy, she would always hold me and say "There There, Tilly, things are not all that bad" although this time there was not mention of things not being so bad, she must have felt that was not the case today.

The kettle clicked itself off and releasing me she poured the hot water onto the coffee and put on the lid, she took my hand and pulled me gently into the living room and onto the settee then disappeared, returning a few seconds later with the cafetiere and two mugs on a tray. She had even managed to put a tiny doily on a plate topped with a few random biscuits - ever the mother I thought and almost smiled but smiling was not possible for me at that moment.

We sipped our coffee, neither of us tasting any of the scalding liquid. After what seemed like hours, although was probably only a few minutes I put my mug down, took a deep breath and headed into my story.

If I there is one thing about my mother it is that she is a great listener. She sat completely silent as I explained all the things that Simon had done to me, during the bath episode she gently covered my hand with hers which was really calming. At the end of the story we were both squeezing each other's hands.

Suddenly she stood up pulling me with her. "Right Tilly. The only thing to do is go to the police station and get this sorted right away."

I didn't argue because with my mother with me I felt safe, I knew she would be able to sort it, she was a much stronger woman than me. She went off to get her coat and I collected my bag from the kitchen and together we met in the hall, she smiled gently at me, squeezed my hand again and putting her arm around my shoulders ushered me out of the front door.

I didn't want to go back to the police station I had visited before just in case Simon was lurking about although I couldn't see of any reason why he should be, I think I was getting a little paranoid so my mother suggested we went to the one local to my her house. We parked in the supermarket car park next to the police building but I still felt nervous and was constantly checking all the cars around us just to make sure Simon wasn't there watching me.

We were confronted with a stern looking police woman who was standing at the counter, glasses on the end of her nose, pen in hand. She looked for all the world like a cartoon character. I was ready to turn and take flight but my mother smiled at the woman at the same time gripping my hand so I couldn't run. Suddenly the cartoon lady's face softened and she smiled at us. Maybe she had just had a bad moment and we had just caught the edge of it, but anyway she looked totally different once the smile hit her mouth and she said

"How can I help"? She had one of those sing song voices, a bit annoying but at the same time quite comforting.

After my mother had outlined the reason for our visit constable Sarah Burgess, well that was the name on the nameplate on the counter, took my name and address and ushered us into a small room a few doors down the corridor. A very basic room in which there was only a table, two chairs and nothing else, she politely asked us to wait there and that she would send someone who would take my statement. We sat and waited for about five minutes until a tall very young but very efficient looking policeman breezed into the room carrying a folder, which I assumed was for him to take my statement. He sat opposite us and opened the file and as he did so I saw that my name was staring at him from the statement paper inside. I glanced at my mother and realised she had seen the same thing, she was staring at the paper too.

"Good afternoon" the young policeman broke the silence "I understand your name is Matilda Waterson, is that correct?"
I then realised that the paper he had in front of him wasn't to take a my statement but was information given to him by

what must have been Simon, as he was the only person who ever called me by that name.

My mother looked at me puzzled, "Matilda ? Who on earth calls you that, your name is Tilly and has never been anything else." Then turning to the young policeman added, "This isn't Matilda Waterson, her name is Tilly."

"Don't worry mum", I said "This must have something to do with Simon as he is the one who calls me that name when he is angry ", then turning to the policeman I continued "I have a feeling I am not going to like what you are about to say next am I right ? "

The policeman looked down a little sheepishly at the paper in front of him the raising he head and looking directly at me he composed himself and hardened his eyes as he said "We have a statement here from a Mr Simon Wheltes who has accused you of assaulting him in his flat at approximately 2.30pm today. I am sorry but I typed your name into our computer and it was flagged in his statement. Now he doesn't wish to proceed with any charges at this time as he is sure it was just a one off domestic but he wanted it put on record that it had happened in case there were any more altercations of similar nature. Now I don't have to arrest you or anything but you must be aware that it has been put on record and if there are any further occurrences of this nature charges may be brought against you, do you understand?"

Both my mother and I sat there totally in shock, how could he have gone to such lengths? I knew the answer immediately, it was so bloody obvious that he wanted to cover himself in case I tried to lay some charges on him. Calmly and without the hysteria I was feeling inside me, and trying to quieten my mother on the occasions she tried to defend me I explained to the officer exactly what happened, why I was there and just why I thought Simon was trying to get in first with his story.

Even when he studied the marks on my face I wasn't sure he was really believing my side of the story. I suppose as Simon had got in first my version seemed like an afterthought, like I was just doing it as a tit for tat.

We left the police station totally bewildered and feeling very let down. The policeman had offered to take down my side of the story but had made it quite clear that he was going to do nothing about it at this time, he had said we should sort it out between ourselves and that he was sure by tomorrow we would be back in the flat playing happy families again. He did though allow me to write a small statement saying that I was in fear of this man and wanted protection if a time came when I felt I needed it. Although I am sure the statement wasn't actually going to be put on any file. He was convinced we had just had a bit of a tiff and no more.

Chapter FOUR

Once back at my mother's house and with an opened bottle of wine and two glasses in front of us we both suddenly relaxed. My face hurt but I was not going to think about it anymore. We had decided on the way home in the car that it was all going to be put behind us, well me anyway.

I was going to get my brother Tom to go to the flat and collect my things, I was going to call the landlord and explain what had happened and whether he believed me or not I didn't care I wasn't going to pay any more rent, he was going to have to take it up with Simon.

I decided to stay at my mum's for a while until I decided exactly what I was going to do, probably find another flat the other side of town, well away from the devil, although I didn't want to be too far from work.

I had brightened a little by the time Tom arrived after he had finished bathing his twin boys and helping his wife Cassandra put the little ones to bed.

"What the hell" were his first words when he saw me followed by "I'll go and kill the bastard!" but my mum and I calmed him and explained exactly what I wanted him to do, just go to my flat and collect all my clothes. I gave him a list of personal belongings and of course my grandmother's chicken clock. Eventually he agreed to do as we asked and promised not to get into a fight with Simon. We knew where it would lead if Tom lost it and started on Simon. Simon would win hands down and I didn't want Tom ending up in hospital or even prison!!! He said he would go mid morning the next day when we hoped, anyway, that Simon would be at work. I climbed into my old bed in my old bedroom that night and felt quite good at last, well apart from a very sore face.

I was up early the next morning as I had heard the cat from next door meowing at our back door, she often did that when the next door neighbours were away for a night even when I lived at home, my mum would give her one of the

51

little cat treats she kept in the cupboard especially for such occasions.

I wandered downstairs in my old dressing gown which was always kept in the wardrobe in my old bedroom just in case I visited and stayed over. I went over to open the back door to let Lulu in and as I stretched up to unlock the top bolt I thought I noticed a movement in the back garden. I opened the door, ignoring Lulu as she brushed past me and taking a couple of steps outside I scanned the garden. There was nothing there but I noticed that the bush at the edge of the pathway that led to the wood behind was moving like it had been brushed past. "Must have been the wind", I assured myself, "There is a fence behind and if there was anybody there they would have had to scale the five foot larch lap fence." The fence was very old and rickety so if somebody had tried to scale it, it would probably have given way. No I was sure I was imagining things. I smiled, very gently, due to my still very sore face, to myself at my paranoia and fed Lulu her treat.

I still had another day before I had to be back at work so I thought I would take my mum out for a treat. I was going to start by taking her a cup of tea in bed but was beaten to it by her arrival the kitchen door, fully showered and dressed in her, what she would have called when I was a child, her "Sunday best" and looking for all the world like she was going to the queen's garden party.

"Off out somewhere special mum?" I jested casually

She looked surprised at my jest, "You know I am", then frowned "don't you remember, I told you I was off with the ladies guild today to the Chelsea flower show and then off for a special celebration lunch, Oh I am so sorry to leave you today of all days, if you would rather I stay here I will."

I could almost see the plea on her face, that I would say "No, of course you must go", which of course I did say. I must admit I did feel a bit let down but would certainly not let her see that. She had been a brick for the past few hours and she certainly didn't deserve to miss a day out just because "the devil" had upset my life.

I gave her a hug and waved to her at the front door and wished her a wonderful day as she got into the taxi she had ordered, probably so she could have a few glasses of bubbly and wine at the lunch, I fully suspected. I went back into the kitchen, checked the clock on the cooker, it was 9.45am - too early for my brother to be at my flat collecting my things so I went up to the bathroom, ran a hot bath with loads of bubbles in it then settled gently. It felt a lot safer than the last time I had done the same thing at my flat.

I must admit I did check the door about a zillion times though, just in case the devil was coming in armed with my laptop, but of course I was being paranoid again, I had made sure I locked the front door after my mother left. As I sank into the relaxing warmth of the water, I closed my eyes briefly but suddenly heard a sound downstairs, sitting up abruptly I listened again, thinking maybe I had dzed off for a second and dreamed a noise but I heard it again, this time louder, a sort of banging.

Climbing out of the bath I grabbed at a towel that was hanging over the radiator and wrapped it tightly around me, still dripping I quietly opened the bathroom door and strained my ears. More sounds. My heart was racing as I very slowly crept across the hall way, listening for any little sound, nothing. Then suddenly another sort of bang. I started to tremble and was torn between reversing back into the bathroom and locking the door or carrying on down the stairs to god knows what! It only took a few seconds for me to compose myself and decide I had to proceed. I don't know why I didn't think of getting dressed beforehand, but halfway down the stairs I realised I hadn't thought of that and grabbed at my towel for reasons unknown - well I suppose for comfort.

At the bottom of the stairs I caught sight of my mother's umbrella leaning against the wall so with my free hand, the one that wasn't clinging for dear life onto my towel, I grabbed it. More noise from the kitchen, this time a sort of scraping. Feeling a lot safer now with my umbrella in hand I advanced to the kitchen door, pushing it open very, very, slowly I dared to look inside. Relief at what I saw flooded through me. There, sitting at my mother's kitchen table was my brother, a bowl of sugar puffs in front of him and a spoon full of the cereal mid way between his mouth and the bowl.

He seemed as startled as me but we both soon realised who we were and he pushed the now only half full spoon into his mouth and grinned.

"Gave you a start did I? Sorry I didn't realised you were in."
he said as he reached for the kitchen roll to mop up the spilt
breakfast cereal, "I went to your flat early and hid in the
garden, I was hoping to see Simon come out so I could
catch him unawares at the gate and tell him exactly what I
thought of him." At this I tried to interrupt him with my
speech about not causing any more trouble but he shushed
me with a wave of his hand and continued, "but he didn't
come out....I waited for ages but then the lady next door
noticed me when she opened the door to let her cat in. She
said she didn't think he had been home all night, as she
hadn't heard his car revving which was a real bug bear of
hers as he did it every time he parked before switching off
the engine. Also his music hadn't been drifting through her
wall since the day before. I hadn't noticed his car was
missing I must admit, but then I wasn't completely sure
what colour his car was anyway. Well I went into the empty
flat. It was tidy, no washing up or any mess anywhere so I
just picked up the stuff you wanted and here I am!" And
with that he popped another spoonful of sugar puffs into his
mouth.

I was a bit gob smacked for a second but then felt really relieved, and optimistically thought that maybe I wouldn't ever hear from Simon again. I grabbed myself a bowl and joined Tom at the kitchen table and poured myself a bowl of the cereal, my mother always kept a packet in her larder just in case one of us fancied a bowl, she never ate them herself but ever since we were little it was our favourite. Tom smiled at me and said "Maybe you should go and put some clothes on first?"

Together we went through all the things Tom had collected for me including my grandmother's chicken clock which I got Tom to fix up on my mother's kitchen wall but as I stood back to look at it I noticed that the beak on the ceramic chicken at the top of the clock was broken. "Oh, what a shame" I thought, but I didn't want to say anything to Tom as he had done me a good favour in collecting everything and I didn't want to blame him for being careless in packing the clock. I just thought to myself I would get a tiny pot of ceramics paint and touch it up so it wouldn't notice.

Then Tom took me back to where my car was parked outside my flat. Luckily there was no sign of either the devil or his car and mine was no longer blocked in so I got in it quickly and drove back to mum's house closely followed by Tom just to be sure I got back alone!

Chapter FIVE

By the time my mother got home that evening I was feeling much better. My face was not half as sore as it had been, probably due to my mood picking up. I had most of the things I wanted from the flat, the rest I decided could bloody well stay there, just as long as I never had to see Simon again I thought it was a small sacrifice.

I knew my mother was eating out at lunch time but I still thought I would take her out for a meal to make up for yesterdays fiasco so I booked a table for 8.00pm at an Italian restaurant I knew she loved. She was delighted to see my mood had improved and still being on a high from her great day out was over the moon to be going out again with me this time for dinner. I also think the few glasses of wine she had drunk at the lunch had assisted with her happiness but who was I to mention it?

The restaurant wasn't too far from her house so we decided to walk so we could both have a little wine, or rather in her case a little more wine.

It was a beautiful meal, I hardly noticed my face hurting as we munched away on garlic dough sticks followed but wonderful ravioli stuffed with ricotta and spinach finishing off with a rather too large portion of tiramisu and an Irish coffee and we covered all the topics we possibly could cram into one meal.

How she had really enjoyed being with her friends at the flower show, the lunch and how she still missed my father but hadn't closed the book on ever meeting a fellow loner of the opposite sex. It made me smile and happy to know that she hadn't just settled to living in Gods waiting room, she had loved my father with all her heart I know but he died five years ago when he was only just 60 leaving my mum a widow at only 58. It was at least 18 months after my father's death that my mum had even started to take an interest in life again but now I can see she is really beginning to enjoy herself. "I love you so much mum" I thought as I looked at her sipping her Irish coffee. I really hope I eventually find a lovely man that I can love as much as you loved dad.

"So what are the thinking of doing now?" She broke through my thoughts suddenly "Of course you are welcome to stay at my house for as long as you like you know that don't you"

"Of course I do mum" I replied "maybe I'll stay for a couple of weeks, just until I can find another flat, as far away from Him as possible though, mind you it will need to be fairly close to work as I might have to sell my car to get a deposit together"

"Oh don't worry about that" she said " I can always help you out with a few pounds for that" and saying that she put her hand on top of mine and squeezed, "I love you sweetheart and will do whatever I can so you never have to be near that awful bully ever again".

I smiled and squeezed her hand back, I felt safe at last.

We linked arms as we walked home and giggled at a slightly drunk man who was staggering a little and trying very hard not to fall over in front of us by grabbing at the fences as he passed. I felt she was more like a sister than my mother.

I used the key she had given me to open the front door but although it was a mild night felt a chill as I walked into the hall. A tiny draft was coming in through the kitchen as I opened the door. I thought maybe I had left the kitchen window open but once inside realised I hadn't left it open, it was actually smashed. There was glass all over the work top and floor. As I glanced around the kitchen to check there was nothing missing, Mum followed me in.

"What the hell has been going on here?" she squealed, "I bet that was the kids from the house next door, there is always something when Wendy's grandchildren come to visit her, balls over the fence, frisbees flying all over the place. I bet they threw one of those things and smashed my window!"

I looked around the kitchen again for a ball or frisbee but spotted nothing until something made me look up at my precious chicken clock, it was no longer missing its beak, it was missing its entire head!

"He's been here mum" I said and started to shake.

We sat opposite each other at the kitchen table, both cradling our cups of coffee my mum had made.

"So what do we do now" my mum eventually broke the silence "why would he just break in and break the chicken's head off"

"Because he's bloody raving mad!" I almost shouted at the stupid remark she had made but stopped myself in time, after all it wasn't my mum who had put me into this rage. "There has been no rhyme or reason to anything he has done to me, he's just fucking crazy. I'll have to move from here, mum or you will be his target too. All the time he knows I'm here he'll continue to goad us both. He knows I love that clock, he's just going to do little things to upset me, or maybe worse." I shivered at the thought, "Suppose this is just the beginning and he plans far worse a fate for me ? Or even you?"

"You must go to the police again" my mother was saying, "Tell them you are worried."

"Oh yes", I replied far too sarcastically, "they would love to hear about him coming in here and breaking the head of my ceramic chicken clock!" I almost laughed at my statement.

"They didn't really believe me last time and certainly wouldn't put out an arrest warrant for a broken chicken head."

Whether it was that daft sentence that calmed me down or the catch up of the wine but I looked at my mother and we both burst out laughing.

"Right" I said, " this is the plan. " Tomorrow I will go to the estate agents, find a flat and be out of here within the week We will get the window fixed, and I will go to the rescue home and get a dog, a big dog ! Now we will have ourselves a brandy, check all the doors are locked and go to bed. I doubt he will come into the house tonight with us here so the window will be OK. I'll put a tin tray up against it just in case, then at least we would hear him if he tried to come in".

After our brandy my mum went off to bed, I didn't feel anywhere near as calm as I would have her believe though, I was scared shitless if truth be known. I had a horrible feeling that just trying to rile me was the beginning of his torture but I certainly didn't want my mother becoming paranoid like me. If I move out he will know I've gone as I am sure he is watching me. I just have to go somewhere he won't find me. I propped up the tin tray and barricaded it in place with a small stool my mother had for standing on to reach up to the top cupboard, then on top I piled books and anything reasonably heavy. I would surely hear any movement. After that I went upstairs and got my duvet and returned to the lounge, curled up on the sofa and tried to sleep.

The sun woke me early, blazing in through the window and for a moment I couldn't remember where I was then suddenly realised and got the sinking feeling you get when you remember something is wrong. I got up and checked the window in the kitchen, nothing had moved, the birds had started singing in the garden and as I dismantled my window barricade I watched the tiny creatures hop from one bush to another and thought just how they have no troubles, well apart from the cat that is and how nice it would be to be a bird.

My mother suddenly appeared in the doorway asking if I would prefer tea or coffee. My mother, so calm, so sweet but probably worried silly inside. I agreed to have some coffee and toast but not until I had gone upstairs for a shower.

As I stood under the flowing warm water I started to feel a little better, my face was not anyway near as sore now which helped and of course I had formed my plan, as soon as I had eaten my toast and drunk my coffee I thought I would head down to the estate agent and see what was on offer for rent. I turned off the water and stepped out of the shower but before I could dry myself completely there was a loud scream from the kitchen. Grabbing a towel and wrapping it around my dripping body I rushed to the top of the stairs and called Mum.

She came to the bottom of the stairs and looking up at me with startled eyes she said "There was somebody in the garden – it was HIM Tilly, he had a horrible mask on, you know one of those rubber ones that covers your entire head, but I know it was him. He had those blue jeans with the frayed holes that he always wears, he was just outside the broken window staring in then he ran off once I screamed."

"Come up here mum" I said "while I dry off, then we'll go down and check he has gone, I am sure his is just doing it to be a shit. I doubt he will come in the house with us both here, after all if he tried to attack me you would be a witness and he wouldn't have that."

She came up the stairs and I could see she was very shaken, she sat on the end of the bed not saying a word while I dried off and got dressed then said "It was horrible Tilly, he just stood there and starred with that grotesque mask, I think he is really crazy, you are going to have to do something about him"

"I know, I know" I replied but just what I was going to do was beyond me at that moment. "Why don't you go and stay with Tom for a while" I suggested "I'll go and stay with my friend Izzy until I find a new flat, I'm sure she won't mind me for a week or so, he will have no idea where either of us is then."

I could see relief wash over her, "OK then" she said "but we'll get somebody out to fix the window first." With that we both went downstairs and she made the coffee and toast.

"He's not going to trouble us any more", I said with very little conviction.

I telephoned work to say I wasn't feeling very well and wouldn't be in for a few more days and then called a glazier to come and fix the window. Luckily he said he could come out within the hour. I then telephoned my brother, he had left for work but his wife Cassandra said of course my mother must go and stay with them, she offered me to go as well, but I thought as they only had one spare bedroom it was unfair to put them out any more and was convinced my friend would be happy for me to bed down at her place for a while.

Next I phoned Izzy. To my surprise she wasn't as keen as I thought she might have been, it was almost like she was making excuses. Eventually she agreed but I wasn't sure she was really wanting me there. I said I would be round at her place that evening if that suited her. I knew she didn't finish work until 5.30pm so I asked her if 6.00sh be OK, she hesitated but then agreed but said she had plans to go out so would only be popping in to change before going on her date.

"Oh, I can't wait to hear all about your new man then," I had said. I knew she had been going out with Harry for some months and was very keen but he had finished it a couple of weeks ago but now to be going on a date meant she had a new man in her life so I was keen to hear all about it but all I got was a grunt.

The glazier arrived as promised within the hour and did a first class job on installing a new glass in the kitchen window. I made him a cup of coffee, paid him and he was gone within an hour. My mother packed a few things and drove to my brother's house. It was only about twenty minutes drive away. I said I would get my things together and follow her there, mainly as I wanted to kill time until I went to Izzy's but also I wanted to see my two gorgeous nephews and have a chat with Casandra about Simon.

I collected as many belongings as I would need for my short stay with Izzy and put them in the boot of my car. I also lifted my chicken clock off the wall, wrapped it in newspaper and put it under the bed, my old bed, the one I always use when I stay with my mum, then I checked the back garden for any signs of "him" of which there was none, locked all the doors and windows and then headed out to my brothers house.

I spent a lovely afternoon with my mum, Cassandra and the boys, we took the boys down to the park where we threw bread for the ducks and then put the kids on the children's swings and watched them giggle as we pushed them back and forth. I almost forgot all my worries for the short time in the park and it was lovely.

Once back at the house my mother took the boys up to the bathroom for their bath which left Cassandra and me in the kitchen with a coffee and slice of her delicious homemade fruit cake.

"Right" she opened with." Just what is going on?"

I told her the story, although my brother had filled her in a little when he headed off to get my stuff from the flat, but she wasn't aware of everything else.

"You should really go to the police" she said once I had finished telling her.

"But just what can they do? "I said. "I mean he hasn't actually threatened me since the event in my flat and he went to the police first which makes me look guilty of attacking him. I really don't think the police believed me anyway. I think he is now pissed off with me and is just trying to frighten me, I am sure he will grow tired of it eventually and move on to his next victim." Although I wasn't entirely sure I believed it myself. "Anyway," I continued, "Mum will be here and he doesn't know where you live and I will be at Izzy's, so once he sees there is nobody at mother's house he will get fed up and go away"

Cassandra sighed. "Well if you believe that well that's fine but I still think you should tell the police just in case"

"OK, if he does anything else I will" I replied " but so far all I have is a broken chicken clock and a masked man at a window, that probably isn't really enough for them to even think about any action."

"Well when you put it like that I suppose you're right, but if there are any more episodes of anything promise me you will tell the authorities."

I promised and taking another slice of her delicious cake settled back on my stool just in time to welcome the twins bouncing into the room smelling wonderfully of Johnsons baby bath and wearing their beautiful Thomas the Tank engine pyjamas.

My brother came in from work and immediately picked the boys up one in each arm and planted a kiss on each of their tummies making them squeal with delight. I couldn't help thinking to myself this should have been Simon and me, having a family, loving each other, our children and life itself, instead of...oh what was the use of dreaming, it was never going to happen with him now. Plonking the boys on the play mat Tom kissed Cassandra, followed by my mother and then me.

"OK, Sis" he said and ruffled my hair, "has the "devil" gone back to his hell hole?"

Before anybody had a chance to speak I jumped in with "Yeah, gone for good I would say!"

Cassandra and mother both looked at me but I just smiled and my eyes pleaded for them to keep quiet. I certainly didn't want my brother charging around to the flat to challenge Simon and resurrect the aggro all over again, especially when deep down I really did hope it might actually be over.

It was just 6.30pm when I arrived at Izzy's flat, she opened the door after the first knock.

"I am so sorry to be a pain" I got in first as I walked into the tiny hall way, "but I wouldn't ask if I wasn't desperate."

Izzy smiled and ushered me into the little and very untidy sitting room.

"You can pop you bags in there" she said pointing to the little cupboard in the corner of the hall on the way in, "and there is bedding in there for you to put in here."

The flat was tiny, admittedly, but as we were such close friends I had visions of us having a bit of fun during my stay. We had known each other since infant school and had remained close through all the teenage traumas, boyfriends and problems of growing, up. But she seemed distant. I was obviously going to have to sleep on the couch which was really tiny to match the surroundings. I had thought we might blow up the inflatable bed and I would just muck in with her in her room. Something wasn't right but I didn't want to annoy her so I said "That will be great, thank you so much Izzy, now tell me all about this date you have tonight?"

For a second or two I thought she was going to tell me, her look brightened and she started with "Well I met........" then she just shrugged and said she had to get ready, so to please excuse her, make myself at home and help myself to anything I fancied from the fridge. It was strange as she was being half her old self and the other half distant, almost hostile.

I decided not to say anything except, "Have a good time, maybe when you get back you can tell me all about it!"

"Oh there is no need for you to wait up you know" she almost growled "I might be late, I'll be quiet so as not to wake you" and with that she closed her bedroom door, re-appearing ten minutes later looking lovely. She gave me a brief smile and then was gone.

I sat for a while wondering what I had done wrong but could think of nothing so I decided I would pop out and buy a bottle of wine, wait up for her to return and then ask her exactly what the matter was. After all we had been friends for so long I could not believe that anything could be so bad that it could come between us!

It was gone midnight when Izzy eventually returned, I was sitting on the sofa with two glasses and a bottle of white wine sitting in front of me on the coffee table, She crept in thinking, I suppose, that I would be fast asleep and she looked surprised with the sight that met her.

"OK" I started, before she had time to even walk across to her bedroom, "Sit."

She looked at me for a few seconds and then did as I requested. I poured two glasses of wine and handed one to her which she took almost too readily.

"Now" I began" just what the hell have I done to upset you, you obviously don't want me here but I think we have been friends long enough for you to go give me an explanation"

She sipped at her wine, then took a big gulp and looked straight into my eyes "I am seeing Simon" she said. "Your ex Simon" and waited for my response. It took a few seconds for me to digest her words and then I looked at her with amazement.

"And that is why you were so off with me? I couldn't give a shit if you are seeing Simon, you can see who you like."

She visibly relaxed at my words "I know you and he had your problems and I know that you hurt him badly mentally as well as physically but he has forgiven you and bears you no ill, but he knows there is no future between the two of you even with you begging to go back to him. I was just worried it might break our friendship if you knew he was seeing me when you still wanted him. I am so sorry but we get on really well and if you can find it in your heart to let me have him and still be my friend then we can be as before."

I was speechless for at least a minute, although it seemed like a lifetime.

"How long have you been seeing Simon then?" I managed to blurt out eventually "I mean we have only been apart for a couple of days."

"Yes it was the day before yesterday. I bumped into him at the sandwich bar in the town and he said that he had left you but that you were begging him to come back but that it was not going to work, then he asked if I would like a coffee after work and it went on from there. Tonight was our real proper first date. I was worried you would be upset with me, please say you're not".

I almost laughed. Well I would have, had the circumstance not been so serious.

"Just what did Simon tell you happened between us" I asked her.

She took another gulp of wine and then said he had told her that he had come home from work early and had cooked me a special meal to surprise me, but that I had come home in a foul mood and started a big row which had ended up with me attacking him. He told her it wasn't the first time I had attacked him but it had to be the last so he had said he would leave, but that I had begged him to stay. He was frightened that I would go out of control again so he thought it best that we split up, at which I supposedly walked out.

I just sat there, shell-shocked to say the least, then told her the full story and finally I lifted my hair so she could see the marks on my face, not sore now but still very evident.

"And how do you think I got these?" I finished with.

"I er... I don't know" she stammered, "Oh my god, was he lying to me? Tilly, was it he who hit you and not the other

77

way round?" It was like a light had suddenly gone on in her head and she reached forward and hugged me. "How could I have been so stupid to believe him against you, for goodness sake you are my best friend, it was just a rebound thing after splitting up with Harry. I was just flattered I suppose that somebody else wanted to take me out, enough of this wine - I have some brandy in the kitchen. Let's have a glass of that and please, please, forgive me."

We sat for a few moments sipping at the rather too large brandies Izzy had poured us, eventually she leaned forward towards me and taking my hand and with a real sadness in her eyes she said "Are we all right now Tilly? I mean really all right?"

I squeezed her hand back and said "Of course we are, remember when we were thirteen and had just started to grow up we made a pact, never let a man come between us...well a boy in those days of course!" and with that we smiled at each other. "We've come a long way since then" I said, "but I must ask you, after everything I've told you is there any chance you are going to see Simon again?"

I was expecting a violent "NO of course not!" but she hesitated before saying quietly, "probably not" and I was shocked to say the least, after all we had just gone through But I knew how upset she was when Harry dumped her so I thought maybe she is still on the rebound.

"You know he might hurt you if you see him again" I tried to tell her as gently as possible "I was not making any of this up you know."

She released my hand and looking at me said, "I will just see him one more time to tell him it isn't going to work, then I won't see him again...I promise."

I wonder if she had her fingers crossed just like we did when we were thirteen, I didn't look to check!

It wasn't until I was tucked up under the duvet on the settee that it suddenly dawned on me that if Izzy had been talking about me to Simon she had probably also told him that I am staying with her. I crept into her bedroom to ask her but all I could hear was the gentle rhythm of her breathing. She was obviously fast asleep,so I thought my question could wait until the next day.

Chapter SIX

When I woke up the following morning Izzy had already left for work. She had left a mug next to a jar of instant coffee and the warm kettle on the counter in the kitchen with a note propped up against it which read "My dear Tilly, I am sorry I had to rush off but I didn't want to wake you just to say good morning, I will be home about six-ish and we can maybe go out and get a pizza or something. I am so glad we are friends again xxxxxxx P.S. you can stay as long as you like!"

I was relieved, I thought maybe she had really decided not to see Simon again after all, but I was still a little worried that he now probably knew where I was living. I got showered and dressed and as I switched on the kettle ready for my coffee there was a knock on the door. Thinking it was probably the postman I happily opened the door not giving a thought to anything really.

Just as I started to pull the door open it suddenly came crashing in on me, There was Simon, that evil face of his, the anger was just...just so immense. He pushed me against the wall and holding me by the neck with one hand started raining blows on my head as I tried to duck to stop him punching my face.

"You fucking cow!" he screamed at me. "You fucking evil cow! Did you think you would get away with it, getting Izzy to refuse to see me anymore? Just why did you think you could fuck with my plans eh?" He continued hitting me. I was powerless to stop him as he was far too strong,

"I am going to die" I thought, as more blows landed on the top of my head. I was seeing stars at this point and thought I would pass out at any moment, prayed I would in fact. Then as suddenly as is began it stopped.

He stood looking at my crumpled body against the wall and with a swift kick said "I was only with the stupid bitch to get back at you anyway, oh and for the record you will never get rid of me. I will always be there behind you, you will never be free. And then one day you will die and I will be free of you, yes that's right, you will die...I WILL kill you, you know, but you will never know when to expect it!" And with that he was gone.

I just lay there on the floor for what seemed like hours although it was probably nowhere near that long. I felt sick so crawled into the bathroom and hung over the loo. I retched several times but nothing would come. I was crying, sobbing in fact but as the tears mixed with snot touched my lips I suddenly came to my senses, I stood up then washed my face. There was no real evidence of his attack as all his blows were on top of my head but I had a raging headache. I searched Izzy's cupboards for some Paracetamol or similar but only found one Ibroprofen, still it was better than nothing so I made the coffee I had intended to make earlier and took it greedily like it was my last meal.

I wasn't sure what to do next, whether to go to my brother's house, but did I really want to get my family involved anymore? Simon knew I wasn't at my mother's now so he probably wouldn't bother her again, but he knew I was here now so I would have to move on again.

I don't know just what I did for the rest of the day, I think I must have slept a lot of it because suddenly Izzy was leaning over me smiling and saying " Wake up sleepy head, are we going to go for that pizza or what?"

"Have you spoken to Simon?" I asked.

"I called him when I got to work this morning" she said. "I could see you weren't happy about me seeing him and I decided our friendship was far more important to me than him, after all I hardly knew him really, I told him exactly that, he seemed to understand and was really nice about it."

I almost laughed at this last statement, he was really nice about it...what !!!!!!

"He came here" I told her. "He barged in and beat me up."

Izzy looked confused. "He beat you up." she said, and I could see she was searching my face for evidence. Reading her thoughts I continued, "No not my face this time, my head, he hit me on the head."

It sounded stupid even as I said it, I didn't expect her to believe me but she surprised me by saying "Oh my god you poor thing, can I do anything, are you feeling alright?" Relieved that she obviously believed me even though there was no evidence I gave her a hug.

"I'm fine now" I said. "Let's just forget it and go get that pizza, but I will have to stop at the shop on the way and get some pain killers as I have a really bad headache."

We linked arms as we walked down the street to the Spar shop for my tablets and then on to the Pizza Express on the corner of her road. We managed to get a window seat which I always prefer, something about being close to the outside world makes me feel better, maybe I suffer slightly with a tiny bit of claustrophobia but I have been like it for as long as I can remember. As the waitress came over to take our order I noticed somebody else approaching our table too, it was my boss.

"Hi Till" he said "I see you are obviously feeling better" There was an edge in his voice, not like him at all.

"Yes I am thank you" I said, "I'll be back at work tomorrow."

"Oh I don't think so" he said "after the letter you sent I don't think you are actually the type of person I thought you were and I certainly won't be expecting you back."

"Whaaat letter?" I was gob smacked. "I have never sent you a lette!"

"Well it certainly looked like your signature. OK the letter was done on a computer but I recognised your signature straight away" he looked shocked at my response and horror. He sat down next to me, fished in his pocket and produced the offending article. "I didn't think you would do such a thing when I first read it but then the phone call from your boyfriend, saying he hoped I received it and that you were staying off sick until I addressed all the concerns you had listed in it."

I took the letter from him. It was awful, it said how he was always taking me for granted, how I wasn't going to put up with it any longer and if he wanted me to work any later than my normal set hours he was going to have to pay me, and then to finish off it said if he didn't agree to my terms I would go to his wife and tell her he had made a pass at me and that I was going to report him for sexual harassment.

"Mr Clever, just how long have I worked for you?" I asked him. "Do you not know me well enough to know I would never write or even think such a thing? If I had any problems with you or work I would have come straight to you about it. I did not write this letter nor did I ask my boyfriend to phone you. In fact my boyfriend and I are no longer an item, he has been unbelievable to me since parting company, including beating me up. It must have been him doing all this, please you must believe me."

His face softened "I am so glad I saw you tonight, I didn't want it to be true and I couldn't see any reason why it should be, but it seemed a genuine letter and then the phone call..."

He took the letter from me and before I had time to stop him he tore it up and gave it to the waitress. "Dispose of this in the pizza oven for me would you please, there's a dear," and then turning to me said "You take as much time as you need to sort this out Tilly, if he troubles you any more you must come and tell me and I will sort it out. I am assuming you have been to the police?"

I explained that I had done but that they weren't very helpful.

"Well as I say if you have any more trouble let me know, I know you don't have a dad to protect you so I will be his stand-in if you like. Now girls, enjoy your meals and I'll see you Tilly when you are ready. OK?" and with that he was gone.

"What a lovely man" Izzy said once he was out of earshot. "I wish my boss was a bit more like him."

"You're right I'm very lucky" I said "Now what shall we have to eat "?

We chatted our way through a ton of garlic bread, a litre of red wine and then a pizza each, I think all the recent upsets I had gone through had made my appetite even bigger than usual, or maybe it was the relief of settling things with Izzy, or my bosses' reactions. I felt like a stuffed pig by the time we left the restaurant but I did feel quite content. We strolled in silence back towards Izzy's flat, I suppose we were both too full up to bother to talk. We were just approaching the front door that led into the main building where Izzy's and the other eleven flats were when we heard a noise from behind, we both swung round together to be faced with Simon, not angry Simon but a smiley Simon, looking how he used to look when I first fell for him, slightly bashful even.

"Hi girls" he started." I'm sorry, I didn't mean to startle you. I was just passing and saw you coming down the road. Err, I wondered if I could have a word with Izzy, if you don't mind Tilly? I, err, mean...well over here Izzy please."

I was so shocked I didn't know what to say but Izzy smiled at him and walked with him into the tiny garden at the side of the front door leaving me standing alone. She returned after a few minutes with a grin on her face.

"What the hell did he want?" I asked rather more severely than I intended, her face changed in a flash.

"I don't think that is really any of your business" she said harshly, "but if you must know he was apologising for anything he had done to make me not want to see him anymore. When I phoned him earlier to say I wasn't going to see him again I had just said that it might upset you, I didn't tell him all the things you had told me about him as I wasn't sure at the time."

"But ...Izzy!" I interrupted her. "He came round to the flat this morning and hit me, surely you believe me now....well you said you did!"

"Oh I know" she said "but did he really ? I mean could you have imagined some of it? I mean when he came up to us just now, did he look like the type of man who would do things like that? I'm not saying you were lying but maybe exaggerating, I do believe you that he came round but he said it was just to talk to you, to explain that he was going to ask me out again and that you just went berserk and tried to hit him and all he did was try and clam you down by holding your arms. After all Tilly, it was quite a coincidence that he hit you where there was no evidence."

"and before that?" I added, "the marks on my face where he laid into me, was that my imagination too?"

She didn't respond to this statement, just turned to open the front door.

"So are you going to see him again?" I asked, but got no response. Whatever spell he had cast on my dearest friend was cast. I felt there was nothing I could do to break it, not at this point anyway. All I could do was move on and hope he treated her better than he had treated me. I was going to tell her exactly what he had said to me this morning about only being with her to get at me. But I thought - what was the point? Once she was under his spell I would only anger her if I try and talk her out of it, and obviously she would choose not to believe me anyway. I thought and had hoped our friendship was a lot stronger than that but it seemed not. By the time I was out of the bathroom Izzy had gone to bed closing her bedroom door on herself.

The next morning once she was out of the flat I got up, packed my few bits and pieces, left a quick note for Izzy saying I hoped her life would work out well but I couldn't help adding a PLEASE BE VERY CAFEFUL OF SIMON at the end of it and a few kisses, and then headed off once again.

I drove into the town and parked in the supermarket car park, put a pound into the machine for two hours parking and went into the shop. I bought a local paper and took it into the coffee bar at the back of the store where I bought a large coffee and a piece of apple pie, not the best breakfast but I just love apple pie. I took a seat in the corner where I wouldn't be too disturbed by the mothers with their push chairs and prams and little toddlers, I had nothing against them but I really needed a bit of me time to sort out just what the hell I was going to do. I didn't want to go back to my mother's house just in case "the devil" put in another appearance; she certainly didn't need the aggro of him being in the background. I decided I would telephone her in the morning and tell her to stay at my brother's for a few more days before she went home just in case. Once he knew I had left Izzy's he might think I would go back to her house but if he was watching the place he would soon realise I wasn't there and would probably leave her alone.

Now, what was I going to do? I opened the paper at houses for rent and there as if by magic was an advert that I felt had been put there especially for me. It read, "Wanted...sharer for house near the centre of town, male or female, own en-suite room and use of kitchen and lounge. Immediate vacancy, Telephone...... and it gave a mobile number.

It took four rings before a man answered.

"Hello?" was all he said.

"Er, I am calling about the ad in the local paper for the sharer." I waited, but nothing. "I was wondering if I could come and see the room?" I continued. "I could come any time today."

The voice on the end of the line suddenly jumped into action. "Sorry for that, I was driving and had to pull over. Yes that would be good if you could come today, I have four more people to see but you are the only one who said they could make it today - so you might just be the lucky one. I'm Mike by the way. Mike Commings."

He sounded really nice. He told me the address and we arranged to meet at 2.00pm. I switched off my phone and suddenly felt really elated. I ordered a second piece of apple pie and another coffee and closed the paper, I had a really good feeling about this meeting, I just hoped I was right.

Chapter SEVEN

I arrived at the address he had given me well before two o'clock so I would have time to have a little walk around the area. I wasn't too familiar with it but soon realised it would only be a fifteen minute walk from work if I moved in here and ten minutes from the main shops and cafes, so a perfect spot really.

I was walking back to my car when I saw a figure getting out of a blue Ford Focus right outside the house I was due to meet Mike at. He was tall, very well dressed in a business suit, had blond hair worn quite long and wow! When he turned his head towards me the face that met me was, well it would be an understatement to say handsome. I know I blushed although from the distance he was from me I'm sure he wouldn't have noticed; mind you with his looks I am sure he would be used to reactions like that. He caught my eye and his face tuned into a huge grin.

"Hi" he said and waved his hand. "I bet you are here about my advert, I'm sorry I didn't get your name when you called this morning."

I caught up with him and extending my hand to shake his said "Hi, yes it was me on the phone, my name is Tilly, Tilly Mitchell.

"I'm not psychic if that's what you think", he smiled a bigger smile which made his eyes twinkle even more. "I just guessed it was you, you did exactly as I would have done, check out the area to see if it was suitable, am I right?"

"Of course" I replied, then realised he still had hold of my hand. I withdrew it quickly, a little embarrassed, but he seemed not to notice.

"Shall we go in and investigate your new home then?" And putting an arm on my back he ushered me up the pathway towards the front door.

It was a nice looking semi detached, probably built around the thirties but with a few modern updates added. There was a nice big hall with the stairs on the right and one door to the left which I found out was to the lounge, then straight on led to another door to the left leading to a dining room then straight on to the kitchen. There was an extension beyond the kitchen housing a study, small utility room and a downstairs loo. Upstairs there were four bedrooms and a smallish family bathroom, one large master, one small double and a box room, then above the extension was the bedroom, simply huge and with its own bathroom. This, I guessed, was the bedroom for the "sharer" (or rather me as I had already decided I was moving in!). It was a lovely room, better than the master bedroom but I suspected he was using this one for the sharer because it had its own bathroom attached.

After our tour Mike asked if I would like to have a coffee, to which I readily agreed. He filled the coffee machine with water and pressed go and then turning to me said "Have you decided if you want to take the room then? There is just one more thing I have to ask you first - do you like cats?"

As he said this he leaned over and opened the kitchen window and called "Mister Bumble!" Within a second a huge grey fluffy cat jumped through the window and started rubbing around Mike's legs and then mine and with the loudest purr I have ever heard. Mike picked 'Mr Bumble' up and stroked him gently.

"I have had him for years" he said "So if you are don't like cats you will just have to learn!" He was smiling of course and when I told him I loved cats he handed Mr Bumble to me and said "Well?"

"If you are offering it to me then yes I would love to take it" I replied, rubbing Mr Bumble's ears affectionately. He smiled again at me and then, switching off the coffee machine opened the fridge and taking out a bottle of prosecco lifted it towards me as if to say "forget the coffee let's seal it with a drink", but all he said was " You do drink don't you ? I mean if you don't I might have to re think my offer."

Then picking up two glasses from the cupboard he led me out into the little garden where there was a table and chairs. The sun was shining and it was almost like the world was telling me my life was going to change from this moment, things were going to get a lot better. I raised my glass to his and we both said together "to sharing!"

As I didn't have many belongings to get from my mother's house I was back at Mike's before it got dark. I let myself in with the key he had give me earlier and found him in the kitchen chopping vegetables when I arrived.

"Hi Tilly" he said as I entered the room. "Or is it Matilda?" My mood changed as soon as he said that name and I felt sick all of a sudden.

"No!" I almost shouted at him. "My name is just Tilly."

The concern on his face was obvious.

"I'm sorry, it was just a question" he was saying, "I didn't mean to upset you - don't you like the name Matilda? I thought maybe your parents had named you after that children's character or something" then continued "I was just making us some dinner as a moving-in treat, I won't be making a habit of it though I can assure you."

He looked at me, smiling, but could see the I wasn't smiling back so he pulled up a chair and settling next to me asked "What is wrong Tilly?" emphasizing the name Tilly.

At this I calmed and looking straight into his beautiful friendly eyes I said "I have a story, would you like to hear it? I don't mind if you would rather not."

He searched my face for a few seconds then said "Is it a gin and tonic story or would you rather stick to wine?"

This made me smile and agreeing it could be a gin and tonic one I watched as he carefully sliced lemons, fetched ice from the freezer in the utility room, collected a bottle of gin from the dining room sideboard, tonic from the fridge and two glasses from the draining board, then expertly produced two very large drinks. He handed one to me, then moving his chair so he was sitting opposite me across the kitchen table and with his drink placed right in front of him, he said "OK proceed."

It was probably well over an hour before I had finished telling him the entire story as he kept stopping me and prompting me for additional information, and at the end we looked out and realised it was dark.

"I had better get that dinner on or it will be bed time" was all he said. "You take your stuff upstairs and sort yourself out, I have put new bedding on the bed so there's no need to do anything on that score. I'll have the meal ready by the time you are down."

I did as he suggested and unpacked a few of my belongings and wondered if he was thinking just what had he let himself in for, letting me move in.

It was at least twenty minutes before I ventured downstairs to be greeted on my way down by a wonderful smell of garlic and roasted vegetables. I wandered into the kitchen just as Mike was dishing up piles of wonderful looking food onto two plates.

"Wow that smells divine!" I said. "You're going to far too much trouble you know, beans on toast would have done."

To which he replied "Oh, sorry, did you think this was for you? No, your beans are nearly hot and the toast is in the toaster, this is actually for me and a friend!"

I stood gobsmacked for a nanosecond before I realised he was really joking.

"Would madam like to sit?" he said and pulled out the chair for me. He then produced a tea towel (supposed to be a napkin) and draped it over my lap. "Would madam prefer white or red?" he said smiling then added "Actually it has to be white as I don't have any red!"

"White is exactly what madam would like" I replied joining in with the fun. We sat opposite each other and started to eat the wonderful meal he had cooked.

After a few mouthfuls and a sip of wine Mike began "Tilly...." Oh no, I thought, he is going to tell me he has made a mistake and doesn't want me here after all? "Tilly I have to tell you something..."

He waited for me to respond which I didn't so he continued. "I have had a bad relationship too, oh not as bad as you, there was no violence involved or anything like that but my heart was broken. I think I am almost over her now but am still very delicate as far as relationships are concerned. I know we will get on, I know you are feeling vulnerable at the moment, I just want you to know that I have no agenda. I am not going to try and make a pass at you or anything like that.......well not unless it happens in time that is" and the twinkle re- appeared in his eyes. "Don't be frightened of me, I will never hurt you in any way I promise." Then to round everything off "I haven't told you what I do for a living have I? Well I am a policeman. You'll have no more worries all the time I am here - OK?"

I could have thrown my arms around him at that moment as the relief came flooding though me like a tidal wave but all I could do was smile and say "Thank you!"

The next day I was up early and ready to start my new life. I thought I would go back to work and in my lunch hour telephone my mother to give her my new address. I went into the kitchen and filled the coffee machine and turned it on, got two mugs out just in case Mike was up while I was still there. I was humming to myself waiting for the toast to pop up out of the toaster when Mike came in.

"Morning" he said not looking quite as bright as he had the night before "I think I drank too much last night, I'm feeling a little heady to say the least this morning, still coffee will sort me out I'm sure." He inclined his head to the almost-ready coffee machine and smiled at me.

"I thought I would go back to work today" I said. "As I told you last night, my boss has been really on my side and will keep an eye on things if he has to."

"And me too," Mike said with a grin, " I don't want to lose my new "sharer" before I even get to know her well enough" he gave me a light punch on the top of my arm and then said he must be off to work now but was looking forward to seeing me later. With that he downed his coffee in one and headed out the door.

I got myself ready for work and locking the door behind me I walked out to my car. I started the engine, but before I could pull away there was a tap on my window. A shiver went through me as I turned to look at who was tapping, to my relief it was a lady wearing a floppy hat and very large glasses. I wound down my window to hear her say "I'm really sorry to bother you my love but if you are going to be here for any amount of time do you think you could park a little further up the road, as my husband is disabled and really needs to be able to park as close to our house as possible. We live next door by the way."

Relief washed over me like a massive wave.

"Of course!" I found myself saying. "I'll leave it a few spaces down in future, I have just moved in and I didn't realise."

She smiled and thanked me, "You'll like living here", she said. "We are a friendly bunch and that Mike is lovely, always looking out for me and my Jim," adding "that's my husband you understand" and was on her way.

I was surprised just how shaken I had been by the innocent tap on my car window. Wow. That bastard must really have got to me, but not anymore, I now have my boss and Mike on my side, I will be taken care of. No more devil to bother me anymore !!!!!!!

It didn't take me long to get back into the swing of things once I got into my office. My boss wasn't in, so I could catch up on the work that had been building up in my absence without being asked to do more. I felt almost normal until Jane from the office next door knocked on my door and walked in.

"Hi Tilly," she said, "I'm surprised you have the nerve to come back to work after all the things you have been saying about us here, does Richard know you've come back ?"

"Of course he knows" I replied, "I spoke with him the other night, but what on earth are you talking about, me saying stuff about you guys? What stuff and to whom?"

"Oh don't come the innocent with me you stupid bitch, you bad-mouthed us all in the pub, we heard all about it, how I am a cow and you could do my job standing on your head with one arm tied behind your back, and how Nigel was an idiot, Clare was a tart. Oh yes, we all heard about you slagging us off, did you think we wouldn't find out? Are you stupid or something?"

Her voice had been getting louder and louder as she was getting more and more angry so by the time she had finished her rant, half the office outside had come to join in or check what was happening.

"I haven't a clue what you are talking about" I said "What pub and when was all this supposed to have happened, and who told you it had?" But before my words were even out of my mouth I knew exactly where all this nonsense had come from. "Don't tell me...I think I know.,. was it by any chance my ex-boyfriend Simon?"

"What if it was?" Jane said.

"And you actually believed him?" I continued. "Jane - all of you -"I looked around to see the faces staring at me. "Just how long have you known me? Do you really think that little of me to think I would say such awful things? Why would I?"

Jane's eyes went down to her feet and she mumbled something I didn't quite catch then when I asked her to repeat it she lifted her head and said "But he was so convincing, and said that you would be leaving us anyway so we might as well hear the truth. I didn't believe it at first but then he said you told him all this and that he wanted to warn us of the person you really are, then when you didn't come into work for a few days we all thought it must be true and you wouldn't be back."

"But I said nothing of the kind, none of it, you must believe me, Simon is an evil man. I haven't been in because he beat me up, you can still see the bruises under my makeup if you look at my face. I finished with him and moved out and he is trying to ruin my life, and obviously you think so little of me that you would believe such rubbish!" I was crying at this point and Jane had her arms around me and was apologising as were the others who had been mentioned in her rant, all saying they never believed him anyway - but of course they did.

I felt really let down by my so called "work friends" but put a brave face on and forgave them all as they left my office. Jane had the last word as she walked out, saying if I need somebody to talk to she was always around. "Yeah", I thought, "but if I need to talk to somebody you would probably be the last person I would choose".

My anger was so great after this little encounter that I couldn't do any work. I went to the coffee machine in the corridor and tried to think of a plan to get my own back on the "devil" but the more I thought about it the more I thought that it would be stupid, he's gone now and that should be the end of it. He must have said all this rubbish a couple of days ago and since then I have seen nothing of him, so leave it. Just leave it.

Things started to take a turn for the better over the next few weeks. I had been out with the girls from the office a few times for pizzas or drinks although it was still a bit strained - we were all making an effort not to dwell on everything that had been said between us. Mike and I were getting on really well, although there was still no hint of any romance between us, we were becoming very close in all other ways. I had learned all about his childhood, how he had always wanted to be a policeman, how his mother had died when he was only fourteen and that his dad had re-married two years later to a very lovely lady whom he respected and loved as far as you could love a step mum. I told him all about my childhood and how my mum was just beginning to start her new life after my father dying.

We sat many evenings at the little kitchen table sharing a bottle or wine and all our secrets. He never tried to make a move on me though, which I was not sure if I was happy or sad about.

Changes began again after about six weeks. I had left the office early as it was a bank holiday weekend and Richard had said we could all leave at three instead of our usual 5.00pm As it was a nice day and I had nothing really special to do I wondered through the park until I reached the little cafe at the far gates where I sat at a table in the sun and ordered a coffee and a spiced bun. Not my usual treat but the buns looked so nice and squidgy I couldn't resist. Taking my kindle out of my handbag I flicked it on and was about to start on the new Lee Childs book I had just downloaded when a voice suddenly broke into my thoughts.

"Hi Tilly how are you?" I looked up to see Izzy standing in front of me. "Is it OK if I sit here?" she was saying as she pulled out the chair opposite me. "I just spotted you and thought I would come and say Hi."

I was just about to say how great it was to see her when a shadow appeared directly behind me and then moved around until it was behind Izzy, then staring directly at me was Simon. Shivers went down my spine but I tried not to show any emotion. He was standing with his hands on Izzy's shoulders and I could see she was trying not to cringe.

"Hello Matilda" he said, in his evil Simon voice. "Long time no see eh?"

Izzy's eyes were pleading with me as if to say "I'm sorry Tilly, really I am."

I just nodded a courteous nod and then moved my attention to Izzy. The more I looked at her the stranger she seemed to look. It took a few seconds for me t realise what it was, she had lots of makeup on - plastered in it in fact, Izzy very rarely wore makeup. Well, maybe a little mascara and lip gloss when she went out, but not thick foundation and eye shadow. She actually looked a bit like a clown, I was about to say something but stopped myself as I saw her pleading eyes. I also thought I saw Simon's hands grip her shoulders a little tighter.

"So," he was saying, "Izzy and I are an item now, so you will have to stop chasing me. I don't want you phoning me or following me around anymore Matilda, we are through and you will just have to accept it."

I was so shocked at his statements I just wanted to get up and smash him with anything I could have laid my hands on but the look on Izzy's face stopped me dead.

"Tell her." he continued addressing Izzy, "Tell her to stop bothering me, she was your friend. "

"Please stop chasing Simon" Izzy said in a cracked voice but her eyes said "Help!" I'm sure. "We are happy together, Simon and me, so please leave us alone."

As I studied her face I realised that the makeup was covering what looked like blue bruises. I had no intention of starting a fight as I felt Izzy would come off the worst so I just stood up and said I had to go.

As I walked away I was thinking I must try and get Izzy away from him as soon as possible, so I would need to think how.

I went to the counter to pay and suddenly Simon appeared behind me and whispered nastily in my ear, "Nice house you're living in now, and of course your new man. Good in bed is he? Watch yourself Matilda, things might be changing."

And with that he was gone, almost dragging poor Izzy from the chair. I watched as they disappeared through the park, she was obviously not going with him willingly as she was struggling. I saw him raise his hand and she immediately stopped and walked calmly beside him. I have to get her away I thought. I'll talk to Mike tonight. I'm sure he will know what to do.

I went straight home and waited for Mike to arrive. He had been getting home about 6.00pm for the past few days as he was on a day shift, but 6.00pm came and went, then 7.00pm and then 8.30pm. I expect he has been involved in some special case I was thinking just as the front door opened and in he came.

"Hi Mike" I said brightly, fancy a G&T before you eat?" I had made a chilli and it was cooking away in the oven as I spoke.

"No I don't really fancy one at the moment" he said kindly "I have had a bit of a rough day. I won't bother you with details though but I think I might go and get showered. Maybe when I come down again."

He was up in the bathroom for simply ages and I thought he might have gone straight to bed but then he suddenly appeared at the kitchen door looking much better.

"I think I can manage that drink now" he smiled at me and then "Oh, something smells good, is there enough for moi?"

"Of course" I replied."

I had actually made it for him but wasn't going to tell him anything of the sort. He pulled two glasses from the cupboard and filled them with ice from the freezer, then after pouring two very large gin and tonics sat at the kitchen table.

"I'm sorry I was a bit off when I came in, I know I shouldn't bring the traumas of the outside world into our little home." Hearing him say our little home made my heart race, it was the first time he had ever mentioned an "our" anything.

"No probs" I said. "It's your job to get involved with the traumas of the outside world." I tried to make light of his statement.

"It's just...." he continued, "It's just...well you'll read about it in the papers soon enough or on the news so I don't think I am breaking any confidences in telling you. I had a call from a woman late this afternoon saying she had heard screams coming from the flat next door to hers and said they sounded serious. She said she had heard screams coming from there before but these were louder and more frightening somehow. She said she didn't want to interfere before as it might just have been the television but she felt this sounded more real. Anyway to cut a long story short" he paused at this point and took a big glug of his drink, putting it down he looked straight at me and I could see tears in his eyes.

"The sight I saw when I got there was just horrible" he said. "There was a young woman, beaten so severely she was almost unrecognisable as human from the neck up. The rest of her was just normal, dressed tidily in a track suit, lying on her back like she was just about to do some pull ups or something but her face....well there wasn't one really. It was horrible Tilly, I have never seen anything so bad in my life."

The tears came then. I went to him and put my arms around him and held him tight for what seemed like hours but was probably only minutes.

"I'm sorry about that" he said at last and I stood back letting go but he reached for me again. "I really need this" he said and hugged me."

All of a sudden the words he had just spoken registered in my slow brain.

"What colour was the track suit?" I asked.

"That's a very strange question" he replied."It was dark blue, what on earth made you ask me that?"

I sat down suddenly feeling sick. "Where was this flat?"

I knew what the answer was going to be even before he said anything. I had my fingers crossed and was silently praying that he wasn't going to say...... "Carson Street." I knew without a doubt then.

He said "But why Tilly, do you think you might know the person?"

Now it was my turn to sob, "Was her name Izzy Turner?" I still hoped that he was going to say no but I knew deep down he was going to say yes.

We sat together on the lounge sofa, he had his arm around me and as I told him the story of my meeting with Izzy and Simon this afternoon and his arm tightened around my shoulders. After I had finished he stood and took my hand, "We must go to the station now so I can get all this down in a statement. We have to find this guy before he kills again."

As I was getting my coat Mike got on the phone to his partner and explained briefly what I had told him and Simon's name. He was telling Toby that he would be coming in with me and I could give a description of the guy, so could he call in a police artist to be there in about twenty minutes. We got into Mikes car, it was the first time I had been in it and under any other circumstances I would have been delighted, but not this time.

We were at the station for hours, with me making a statement, giving a description for the identikit picture ready for circulation, and then more detail of the meeting in the park that had happened earlier in the day.

It was well past midnight before we headed back to Mike's house. I felt shattered and so very, very sad. Mike was really quiet on the journey home, then he suddenly blurted out..."That actually could have been you Tilly, I mean if you had stayed with him it could so easily have been you."

A shiver went down my spine at his words but I couldn't help thinking it still might be me, if they don't catch him I might be next. We both entered the house in sombre mood and Mike went straight to the kitchen and taking two brandy glasses from the cupboard poured a large drink in each. No words were spoken for what seemed like ages and then Mike just said very casually "Come to bed with me Tilly, I think we need each other tonight."

It was a surreal night. We were both unbelievably sad but also so very close in a strange way. There was nothing sexual between us it was just two souls comforting each other in their hour of need...or was it more?

In the morning I woke and realised I was alone in Mike's bed. I panicked for a moment not knowing what to think when the door suddenly opened and in he walked carrying a tray with two cups of coffee and some toast. He sat on the side of the bed and smiled kindly at me.
"I thought you should eat something before you face today."
And with sadness in his voice said "I know she was your friend and I am so sorry this has happened but you must realise it wasn't your fault. You were going to talk to me about it I know but you couldn't have been aware that things would go so badly wrong in a matter of hours. Look at it in this light, if I hadn't been on the shift I was on I may have been home earlier and you would have told me about what happened in the park and I might have gone around to see them, or I might have said it is their problem to sort out. We can't blame ourselves when things like this happen, we are all guilty of missing the boat in so many ways every day. We will catch him Tilly and he will go to prison for the rest

of his life, I promise you. Now eat your toast and drink your coffee. We have to go back down to the station to go over everything again."

He picked up his cup and started to leave the room but stopped in the door way just to say "I don't regret what happened between us last night Tilly. I know we both needed each other badly for the wrong reasons but I wanted you for the right reasons and have done for a while now. If you want to move into this room from tonight nothing would make me happier, but it is up to you" and with that he went down stairs.

I think if he hadn't been there that morning, if he had regretted our night together or had felt guilty I think I would have died there and then but he didn't. He was my rock and I had no regrets about the night, I knew I was falling in love with him, I had known for a while and now although I had no right to feel remotely happy after the events of yesterday I did feel happy, happy that Mike was there, happy that he was so caring. I felt guilty as hell for feeling this was but it isn't every day you admit to yourself you are falling in love and it might just be reciprocated.

The next few weeks went in a blur. The police had put out an APB to try and find Simon. They had searched my flat but he had left nothing that would help in tracing him. Mike was wonderful. He held my hand tightly during Izzy's funeral and was very kind to Izzy's parents, assuring them that everything was being done to find Simon and lock him up forever. Although this didn't help how they felt, at least he had made an effort and was really committed to carry out his statement to them. Richard, my boss, had been very understanding too and told me to take as long as I needed to get through it but I had said I needed to get back to work after a couple of days as it was the only thing to do really. Staying at home and moping and blaming myself wasn't going to bring poor Izzy back.

Chapter EIGHT

Mike and I had grown very close during this awful time. I had moved into his bed and we had become a real couple. All thoughts of Simon and our history had started to drift away just slightly. Of course it would never go away and I would never get over what he had done to Izzy but I didn't think he wouldn't dare to be around anymore which made me feel much safer, although that alone made me feel even more guilty. The police had been given a few leads but they had proved useless. Mike thought that Simon had probably gone to ground in some northern city where maybe the publicity which surrounded Izzy's death wasn't so prominent and where nobody would have much chance of recognising him. Especially if he had grown a beard or let his hair grow long and changed his name of course. Mike didn't think he would have gone abroad as the police had sent his details to all airports and ferry ports. On one hand I obviously hoped that I would never see or hear anything about him again, but on the other I really wanted them to find him so he would receive justice for what he had done.

It was several more weeks before things started to happen. It was getting close to Christmas, the shops were getting busy and the fairy lights were adorning all of their windows. People were everywhere pushing and shoving, carrying huge bags from all the big department stores, it was pure hell shopping but also really fun as there were Christmas carols playing in all the stores and the staff were all dressed up with Santa hats or as elves.

Mike and I were squeezing our way through some of these crowds in Selfridges trying to find something suitable for my mum and his step mum. We had no idea of what to get but decided Mike would go in one direction towards the scarves and the like and I would go towards the unusual gift section. We had agreed to meet at the perfume counter with our ideas in half an hour. Then, if all else had failed, perfume it would have to be.

We were both giggling as we "synchronized" our watches, saying "Right - exactly half an hour!".

Off we went in opposite directions, I was still smiling to myself when a man bumped into my side. "Oh excuse me" he said and disappeared into the crowd. I was just about to say "Never mind" when in an instant a searing pain in my side suddenly made me grab at the counter nearest to me. A disgruntled woman started to curse me for pushing her as I grabbed out but then realised as I fell to ground that I had blood all down my side. She screamed and as all the shoppers turned towards me all I saw was a blur of faces staring down at me. And then I passed out.

Apparently I was unconscious for two days after an emergency operation to remove my spleen and repair all the damage that the serrated knife had done to my body, and apparently Mike had hardly left my side during this time.

When I did open my eyes I saw his concerned face leaning over me and his voice very gently saying my name and telling me I was going to be fine. I tried to pull myself up but he very carefully pushed me back down again saying

"Stay still, please, Tilly or you will burst your stitches." It was only when I heard these words that I realised that I was in a hospital bed and as I moved pain wracked my body. "What happened?" I asked him. "All I remember is walking into a department store with you."

Mike told me everything that had happened and that they hadn't caught whoever did this to me. He also told me that the doctors had been very worried for a while, as I had lost so much blood, but that I was well on the way to recovery now. He ended up with asking if I thought it could have been Simon who did this to me. It took me a few minutes to register just what he was saying but I was too weak to even think at this moment in time, I couldn't even remember what had happened. Mike sensed that this was not the time to address the issue so he stroked a piece of my hair from my face, kissed me ever so gently on my forehead and said I was to get some more rest. He was going to go back home for a change of clothes and that he would be back in a couple of hours and that I was to get some sleep and not to worry about anything. I readily agreed to this as I felt as weak as a kitten and so very tired. I lifted a hand as if to say

OK and see you later as he went to the door. I was awake enough to notice though that there was a uniformed police officer standing just outside my door. As I drifted off I did think "Why is he there?"

It was beautifully bright when I woke and I did think for a second that maybe I had died and was in heaven but soon realised I was still in my hospital bed, and although it was December a beautiful sun was shining into my window. Mike was quietly snoring in a chair next to my bed. I felt so much better, the pain I had felt the last time I woke seemed to have subsided considerably, probably due to a drip of something in my arm. A nurse suddenly popped her head into my room and asked if I would like a cup of tea.

"What time is it?" I asked and Mike answered with a sleepy "It's 6.30 darling." The nurse smiled, saying she would bring two cups, and was gone.

"You're looking a lot better Tilly," Mike continued sleepily, and with that he kissed me, this time on the mouth rather than my forehead.

123

"I feel so much better Mike and I think I might be starting to remember things." Mike, more alert now, pulled the chair around so he was right next to the bed.

"Do you think you might be able to talk about it then darling, while it is coming back to you? It's really important if you can, as we need to catch the bastard who did this. He might be off targeting some other poor victim."

It was coming back to me in huge waves, the fun of the shopping, the synchronising of the watches, the laughing together then the man bumping into me.....the voice.....the "Sorry"

"...I knew that voice. He won't be targeting anyone else Mike...it was Simon. I'd know his sick voice anywhere."

The next three days went by in a bit of a whirl. A kindly police man came and took a statement from me - not Mike, as he was too close to me to get involved in the legal side of things, but Greg a constable from a different station. He knew Mike well and was very genteel with me and Mike held my hand all through it.

I was feeling loads better after a week and although the doctor recommended I stay just a few days longer I was dying to get home and back to normal, even if I was still very aware of the pain in my side with every movement. I was convinced that if I was at Mike's house I would recover much quicker. Mike was an absolute saint, he fussed around trying to make me as comfortable as possible It was only a few days until Christmas Eve and I was desperate to try and make sure this was going to be the most wonderful holiday. As I hadn't had time to go and get him a present I had called my mum while Mike was out and asked her if she would go and get him the sweater I know he had admired before the attack. Bless her! She arrived with it wrapped and labelled and I just had time to hide it away before Mike got in. My mum made her excuses for being at the house saying she had popped in to check on me as she knew Mike had gone into work for the afternoon and she was delighted when Mike insisted she stay and eat with us. My mum really liked Mike and was so happy and relieved I had found somebody whom I could trust.

There had been no sightings of the "devil" since my attack and I was beginning to think that maybe, just maybe, he had either left the country or at least gone to ground again, hopefully miles and miles away. The police were still keeping a look out for him although they didn't hold out a lot of hope of catching him. Well, unless he committed another attack!

Well, Christmas was wonderful. Mike and I shared three blissful days together, just the two of us and I fell more and more deeply in love with him. We spent New Year's Eve with my brother Tom, Cassandra, the twins and my mum and apart from the occasional tinge of pain in my side can honestly say it was the best time of my life!

January started off very mild but by half way through it was bitter with frost on the ground most mornings and a horrible wind that cut right through you every time you left the house. I was feeling so much better and had decided I was ready to go back to work. Mike said I didn't need to as he would provide for me but I really needed to get back to normal as soon as I could for my own sanity. Richard my boss had been so very understanding in keeping my job open for me, but I couldn't expect him to keep it open for much longer - so return to work I would.

My first morning arrived and I got up, showered and dressed well before I needed to as I was a little excited. Mike boiled me an egg and cut me some bread soldiers saying as I was the army I needed to march on my stomach and that the bread fingers were my platoon of soldiers. We giggled like a couple of children as we ate our eggs and drank our coffee, then following an incredibly passionate kiss which almost ended up with us going back to bed Mike got into his car and me in mine and off we went to our respective jobs.

It only took me the morning to get back into the swing of things. Everyone was really nice, unlike how they had been when then had been listening to Simon's lies. I think they now all realised that he had made everything up. The day just flew by and in no time at all I was driving my little Renault back to Mike's house, although he had said I was to call it "our" house now. I was almost home when I glanced in my rear view mirror and noticed that the green car that had been behind me since I left work was still there as I turned into my road. A cold feeling went right through me but I couldn't tear my eyes away from the mirror. Suddenly there was a loud hooting and I realised I had nearly hit a reversing car. I just managed to pull out of the way as the car reversed out of a drive, the driver raised his hand as if to say sorry and while this was going on the green car sped past me and disappeared down to the end of my road, I just caught sight of its brake lights as it slowed to turn.

"Stupid idiot" I thought to myself, it was just somebody who happened to be going the same way as me and nothing more. I parked a little down from "our" house, as I had promised the lady next door that I would and was just walking back from my car when I saw the green car again coming back up the road. I stood for a second so I could see who was driving, but suddenly the lady next door came out and started to thank me for remembering to park further down past her house and as I turned the green car sped past again. I missed seeing the driver clearly but I knew exactly who it was and my knees just gave way under me.

Two minutes later I was on my feet and being helped very gently into the house next door where a very startled looking Myra (she told me that was her name) was sitting me down on a chair in her kitchen and within minutes she had put a cup of hot sweet tea into my hands.

"You just drink that up my love" she said. "Did you have lunch today, that is usually the reason people faint, or er are you pregnant?" she smiled and I had to smile back at her concern and totally strange reasoning for me passing out in the street.

"Yes" I said. "Maybe I missed lunch."

Mike got home about an hour later and I had the dinner on the go by that time. I had poured myself a glass of wine which he noticed as soon as he walked in.

"Starting without me?" he joked as he gave me a squeeze and then "Something smells good!" He grabbed himself a glass and started to pour himself some wine just as the phone went. I picked up the bottle and carried on where he had left off while he answered it but as soon as he had listened for about a minute I could see something was wrong.

"When was this?" he was saying. "How bad? Oh my god, I'll come down now". Putting the phone down he came towards me and taking both my hands in his led me to one of the kitchen chairs. He pulled one up next to me, picked my hands up again and started to tell me......."A body was found today in the wood near Cooper's corner, you know where that is?"

Oh yes I knew alright, it was about 500 yards from my office. I nodded.

"Well it was a girl about your age with the same colour hair as you. I wasn't involved in the case but, well Tilly, she had been beaten to death. There was a witness, a lady had been walking her dog when she was nearly knocked over by a man running, she didn't pay much attention to begin with until she heard on the news about a body being found and she has now realised she might be a witness to the murder. She is at the police station now giving a statement. Tilly, she has identified Simon from some pictures they have shown her, she said the man who pushed past her jumped into a green car and drove off. Darling, didn't you tell us that Simon had a green car when you first met him?" This was true although he had bought a different one later - a red Ford - but maybe he had just stored the green one for 'special' use.

We drove in near-silence to the police station, Mike insisted I went with him after I'd explained about the green car episode earlier He said he would feel better if I was with him, something I totally agreed with. I sat in an interview room while Mike went off to talk with his colleagues and later brought me in a cup of tea. I sat there for a while just thinking what the hell Simon was going to do next. It was about an hour before Mike came to get me, by which time my nerves were shattered, but with Mike's comforting arm around my shoulders I started to relax eventually.

"Tilly, let's get you home, I think a big glass of brandy could help don't you?" I smiled weakly and snuggling against his arm told him I thought that would be the best thing now. Once we got home I poured us two large brandies and we took them into the lounge, curled up on the sofa and sat quietly for a few moments.

"Oh my god. That poor girl. Do we know who she was or anything about her?" I said.

"Well, she was twenty-three, she worked at the local delicatessen and she lived with her mother. No father around. Apparently she was a quiet girl but her mother said she had been seeing a man lately and seemed a little on edge a lot of the time. We have to stop him, Tilly. We have to stop him."

We sat there snuggled together sipping our brandy for a little longer, then Mike jumped up and walked all the way through the house checking every door, every window, every catch.

"Tomorrow" he said, "I'm going to get the best burglar alarm I can. That bastard is not coming anywhere near you, don't you worry Tilly. You're going to be safe with me. I'll never ever let anything happen to you, we will catch this bastard, lock him away and throw away the key. You will never have to worry about him again."

Mike insisted on taking me to work the next morning, he said he didn't want me driving on my own again. He told me I must stay at work until he could pick me up, even if it meant waiting an extra hour or so. I must not go out on my own anyway, he said. I had absolutely no problem with this and would have stayed in the office all night waiting for Mike if necessary. I certainly wasn't going to go anywhere on my own with this lunatic on the loose.

Luckily I didn't have to wait too long. Mike said that the trail had gone completely dead on the devil so he had left it to his colleagues to keep searching and if they had any leads they promised to let him know straight away. We drove home making polite chitchat trying desperately hard not to mention his name although Simon would always be on both our minds.

Once in the house things seemed to improve between us, we cheered up, opened a bottle of wine and started to relax a little. "I promise you" Mike said again "We will find him and you will never have to worry about him again". I snuggled up next to him glad of the reassurance and I started to feel safe yet again!

Chapter NINE

Three months went by. Mike and our love grew stronger and stronger. We started to relax and be happy and even started thinking of the future, then on Valentine's Day Mike asked me to marry him and I was the happiest woman in the world. We went out together and chose my engagement ring and went out for a lovely dinner with my brother, his wife and family and my mother. Mike's parents couldn't make it as they were on holiday in Australia but they sent their blessing and said they couldn't wait for the wedding.

Oh my goodness! What a wonderful life I was having, everything was going right at last! I had completely, well almost completely, forgotten about the awful, awful, man and the awful, awful, things he'd done. Nothing had been heard about him for so many months now I started to feel safe thinking he must've gone somewhere miles away and I would never hear about him again. We planned the wedding, September we thought, as everyone will be back from their holidays then.

So the plans began. We decided on a small ceremony in the local church with no more than forty people and then a small reception at a local hotel followed by an evening party where another forty people would join us.

I took my mother with me to buy my dress. I know, it is my mother and usually you would take your best friend - but I look upon my mother as my best friend and I knew that she would help me choose the right dress. I tried on, oh, it must have been at least twenty and eventually chose a cream silk plain but elegant mid-calf dress, with tiny diamantes on the shoulders and edging on the neckline. Now just describing it, it sounds very un-special and boring but it wasn't, it was beautiful. I paired it with a cream and gold pashmina. My mum cried when she saw me come out of the changing room, which was just the reaction I was looking for.

Mike and I did all the wedding favours ourselves, we made little parcels out of all the usual things like sugared almonds and miniature chocolates, we giggled as we sat cross-legged on the floor creating our little contribution to what was going to be our wonderful, wonderful wedding day.

I had told Mike that it's supposed to be unlucky for the bride and groom spend the night before the wedding together, so I insisted he went to stay with Toby who was going to be his best man. "Really?" he said. Toby was Mike's closest friend and partner at work. They had joined the force together, had gone through the training school together and were inseparable in their social life, until Mike had met his last girlfriend. Then they had drifted apart as Toby wasn't too keen on Anna, but since their break-up - and also once I came on the scene - Toby had been around loads. I got on really well with him and I think he really liked me too, so I was really pleased when Mike said he was going to be his best man. He and Toby and a few friends would have a ball at Toby's house once the beers were in.

"So what will you be doing?" Mike asked me, "while I'm getting pissed the boys?"

"Don't get too pissed" I said. "I don't want you to forget where to come the next day"

"No chance of that!" Mike laughed. "I've been waiting for this day for a long time. You don't think I would miss marrying the girl of my dreams!"

I put my arms around him and felt his strong arms around me.

"We're going to be so happy Mike. I know we are!"

"Of course" he replied, "now tell me - what are you going to do the night before the big day?"

"Well I have no idea really, the girls from work are going to arrange something, but I have no idea what, at the moment."

"Well, if it involves a stripping policeman don't go running off with him eh? Oh, and no comparing...er...things !!"

"I love you so very much" I replied, wrapping my arms around him for a final squeeze. "Nothing could ever put me off you...ever" and then added just for fun....."Well if it is a lot bigger than yours..I might just ......" Mike playfully slapped my bum and with that he was gone to meet as arranged with Toby.

As soon as Mike had gone I went upstairs to get ready to go out and meet the girls. I had no idea what they were going to arrange but I was quite excited. I was halfway through sorting out something to put on when the phone made me jump. I grabbed at the one beside the bed, thinking it would probably be Emily from work telling me exactly what time they would be picking me up, as they had kept everything hush hush up until the eleventh hour......

"OK, where are we going then?" I asked brightly as I picked up the phone, but instead of Emily's voice on the other end I got an ugly harsh voice I knew so very well.

"Hello Matilda.....Happy wedding" was all I heard as I slammed the receiver down straight away. I sat for a few moments on the edge of the bed with the phone still beeping beside me, the caller had hung up but I hadn't cut the call. I picked it up with shaking hands and pressed the off button and then threw it down onto the bed as if it was on fire.

Five maybe ten minutes went by before I stopped shaking. How the hell had he got my number? Mike and I were very careful who we gave our number out to. We had it changed after all the troubles but I didn't doubt for one moment that the Devil had ways of finding out things. Then I started to panic - maybe he had been around to see my mother to get my number from her. I grabbed at the phone again and dialled my mother's number, no reply. I called my brother and got Cassandra.

"Oh hi" she answered cheerily, "are you looking forward to your night out tonight? Oh, what am I saying, of course you are, but more excited about tomorrow eh!" She sounded so jolly, I didn't want to worry her so I just said that yes of course she was right, but that I was just wondering if she had seen mum today. "Oh she's here with me Tilly, did you want a word?" then as soon as she finished the sentence I heard my mum's voice.

"Is everything alright darling?" mum was asking, then without waiting for a reply continued with "I thought I would stay with Tom tonight so I could help get the children and ourselves ready tomorrow. We wouldn't want to be late, now, would we?" Oh Mum, I thought, I love you so much and I was so worried. But I obviously didn't say any of this to her, instead I said I was just checking that everyone was organised for lifts etc. She hung up after telling me not to worry and to have a nice time tonight.

I hadn't asked her and Cassandra to come out with us tonight, as it was only supposed to be for a few drinks and a meal somewhere. After all the wedding was the next day so I didn't want a frantic "Hen Do", it really wasn't my kind of thing anyway. I don't mind going to other people's but not for me.

I felt a lot calmer once I had spoken with my mum and my shaking had subsided, although I was still worried about just how Simon could have got our phone number. Just as this thought crossed my mind, the phone rang again. I nearly jumped out of my skin, but I picked it up and then realised that we had caller ID on the phone and it said Emily, when it had rung previously I hadn't even looked at that, but I would certainly check the number out once I had finished my call with Emily. She told me that a taxi would be picking me up at 7.30pm which was still two hours away, plenty of time for me to "get my gladrags on" as she so eloquently put it. As soon as I hung up I scrolled down the phone to see the last caller number but of course it said withheld !!!

I was very tempted to call Mike but then thought why should I worry him tonight of all nights, after all I wasn't going to be here on my own tonight anyway as Emily and two of the other girls, Pippa and Ashling had said they would stay over so we could all get ready together in the morning. I decided I certainly wasn't going to let the Devil spoil my special evening by trying to rile me. I had decided that was his intention. I wasn't taking it mildly obviously, as I know what he is capable of and I should inform the police I know as they are still looking for him, but not tonight. He could have been phoning me from anywhere in the country, the world maybe, and probably using an untraceable throw away mobile so the police wouldn't have a lot to go on even if I did report it. I would talk to Mike after the wedding, I decided.

I went to the kitchen window to call Mister Bumble to come in for his supper but he didn't come after three calls. I shouted to him that he would just have to stay outside until I got home but then felt a little guilty, so I popped his food bowl just outside the back door in case he got hungry before I got back. Stupid really, I thought, as the cat next door would probably come around and eat it and also if Mister Bumble was that hungry he would catch a mouse or something. Still, I had grown very fond of that cat and I did worry about him.

It was nearly 7.30pm and I was ready and waiting for the taxi when I heard the car pull up outside. I grabbed my bag and was just about to open the front door when something stopped me. I have no idea just what, but I put the chain on the front door and the dead bolt then ran to the back and double locked the door also, then peeped out of the front window. There was no taxi or any other car for that matter parked anywhere near my house but I still had this strange feeling I couldn't shake off....then I saw the taxi arrive and started to relax again. It pulled up outside and three giggling girls climbed out wearing bright pink sashes reading "friends of the bride" in huge black lettering. I smiled and ran to open the front door.

"Come on Tilly!" they were calling from the front gate, "Your carriage is waiting!"

I went outside and was just pulling the door closed behind me when I noticed a large box at the side of my front door, covered in pretty wedding paper and sporting a big pink bow on the top.

"Oh look what somebody has left for me!" I squealed for the girls to come and see but they were climbing back into the tax.

"Come on!" they were calling "Hurry up, those cocktails are getting warm!" so I gently lifted the box, which was quite heavy, and put it just inside my front door ready to investigate when we got back. Shutting and double locking the door I ran down the path and jumped into the taxi with the girls.

The taxi took us straight into town and pulled up outside Cobblers Bistro and wine bar where we all jumped out, Emily insisted on paying the driver and booked him to return at 12.30.

"Can't get you home too late" she said, "We want you looking good for tomorrow - and after what we will be drinking tonight you will need a good few hours sleep!"

We all piled into the wine bar where four other girls from work were waiting with cocktails at the ready. Now I know I like a few drinks and I can handle them as good as the next man, but after an hour of non-stop cocktails on an empty stomach I was beginning to feel quite whoosy. Luckily our table was ready and we all sat and had a wonderful meal, which made me feel so much better. The girls were brilliant, they had bought me a joke shop veil with "Bride to be" written on the front and gave me all sorts of daft things such as the usual "L" plates and gaudy garters. I don't know if it was because of our upset at work all those months ago or whether I had just underestimated their friendship, but we had a really great time and I was thinking just how lucky I was to have such good work colleagues as friends.

The witching hour came all too soon as I was so enjoying my night, well we all were I think - we were all pretty drunk. We had popped next door to the night club at about 10-ish but it was pretty quiet so we didn't stay too long, then back to the wine bar for more cocktails and a competition on who could down them the quickest! I think I may have lost on more than one occasion.

Still, we were all just about standing when the nice taxi driver returned and shoehorned us into his cab, then with us all shouting our goodbyes to the other girls we headed back to the house. Of course it was all dark and gloomy when we arrived and we all stumbled giggling up the path to the front door. It took me ages to find the key and then another age to unlock the door but eventually we all fell into the hall.

"Nightcaps for everyone!" I was shouting and throwing my arms up in the air as if ordering them from some invisible slave. Emily tripped over something as we stumbled in, "Oops, sorry!" she said as she tried to move it out of the way.

"It's that present somebody left you Tilly, I hope it wasn't glasses or china as I have just knocked it flying!" We all looked at her and burst out laughing.

"Well if it is glass or china I am going to get the superglue out and make you stick it all back together then!" I joked.

Well we never got around to checking if it was china or glass or whether Emily would have to stick it all together, because Pippa poked her head out of the kitchen door and called "Come on ladies! I have made us all a nightcap.......!" Dreading just what the nightcap was going to be, but too drunk to really care, the three of us staggered into the kitchen to meet our hopefully last drink of the night.

I woke at about 7.00am with a raging hangover. I threw one leg out of bed and tried to follow it with the other but didn't quite make it, falling back onto the mattress and wishing I hadn't had the last at least ten drinks

"...Oh", my head said, "just what have you done to me?" Then suddenly I woke up "...it's my wedding day, what the hell am I doing feeling sorry for myself? Get up, you fool!" I managed to get up at that thought and went into the bathroom, turned on the shower, stripped off my clothes (which I hadn't bothered to remove before falling in a heap on my bed the night before) and dived underneath the wonderful warm water. I felt better almost immediately and even my headache eased off a little. I pulled on my dressing gown once I was dry and started down the stairs, stopping off en route to see if the girls were awake. All three of them had piled onto the double bed Mike used to have until we moved into my old room - it was a better room once we became a couple. They were all snoring and looked really funny all lying in different directions, it looked like there were twenty of them instead of just three. I thought I would

146

leave them a little longer as it was still only 7.30am and the wedding wasn't until 2.00pm so we had simply loads of time.

I wandered down the stairs and into the kitchen, there was a strange smell as I crossed the hall but thought nothing of it at the time. In the kitchen I filled the coffee machine and reached for the aspirin from the top cupboard and as I did so I noticed the phone flashing, indicating there was a message. I popped a slice of bread in the toaster, filled up my cup with the freshly made coffee and sat at the little table, then picking up the phone I dialled the number to pick up any messages. The voice on the phone said "You have five messages."

"Ahh, I thought. People wishing us well, I expect. The first was from Toby asking where Mike was. Funny, I thought, then oh, Mike must have stopped off somewhere on his way over to Toby's and Toby was getting impatient to begin their night - the message was timed only half an hour after Mike had left me. The next message was Toby again, this time an hour later, weird I thought but I still wasn't too concerned. Number three was from my mum saying to have a great evening and that she was so excited about the wedding and giving me all her love. Number four was from Toby yet again saying "Just where the hell are you mate ???" this was timed at three hours after Mike had left me. I was beginning to get worried then, what if Mike had had cold feet and had done a runner? No, I thought, he would never do that to me, he loves me, but why had he missed going to Toby's house ? Then a thought struck me, he did say there would be surprise for me on wedding day, maybe he was sorting that out and it took longer than he had thought. Yes, that would be it and the next message would be from Toby telling me not to worry as Mike had appeared even if it was really late. Number five was going to explain all I was sure.

It didn't. Instead of Toby's calming voice it was a message from the Devil.....

"Did you like the present I left for you, Matilda?" his voice grated on every nerve ending I had in my body. I slammed down the phone just as the girls all filed into the kitchen, I hadn't even heard them coming down the stairs.

"Phew! What the hell is that weird smell in the hall?" Emily said as she came through the door. I swung around to face her with the look of dread on my face.

"I think it might be coming from that present you kicked over last night..." Tears started to roll down my cheeks and Emily put an arm round me asking what the heck was the matter.

"It's your wedding day!" they all chorused, "Why are you crying?" I didn't even think to explain, just walked slowly towards the box which was still lying on its side in the hall. Its pink bow wasn't so pink now...the smell was quite strong and the floor around the box looked a funny colour, as I got closer with the girls all around me we all saw at the same time the discolour on the floor was a dark wet substance. I pulled back and looked at the girls in horror. Emily had tears in her eyes, Ashling was just white but Pippa was on the case.

"What the bloody hell is in it, Tilly?"

"I think it might be something dead" I said and then told them about the message from the devil.

"I bet it's a dead cat or something" Pippa was saying, "do you want me to look Tilly?" I nodded and moved back to sit on the stairs. We all watched.

"Do you have any rubber gloves" Pippa asked, again I nodded and pointed to the kitchen cupboard under the sink. Pippa dashed in and returned with my pink rubber washing up gloves on her hands, then we all pulled back again while she knelt down beside the box.

Emily turned to me and said " He's only trying to upset your day you know Till, he's just a sad bastard."

"No Emily, he's worse than that, he's a killer and he's mad".......just as I said those words Pippa gave an excruciating scream and was sick right there in front of us all. Emily grabbed her and pulled her away from the box. We were all shaking. Only Pippa had seen what was in the box but we all knew it was bad.

Emily took charge. "Let's all go into the kitchen" she said and ushered us through the door, then pulling Pippa back into the other side of the hall way she closed the kitchen door. Ashling and I sat at the table not speaking just staring into space.

"Do you think it is Mister Bumble" I asked Ashling. "He didn't come in for his dinner last night, Oh my god he's killed our cat, hasn't he!"

Then we heard Emily pick up the phone in the hall and speak quietly to whoever was on the other end. I was sobbing by this time and had my head down just as Ashling opened the window and the cat jumped in. Relief washed over me in an instant and I grabbed the cat and held him tight.

"But if it wasn't Mister Bumble then what was it?"

Emily came back into the kitchen and shaking like a leaf poured out some coffee and put a cup in front of each of us. "Where's Pippa?" I said. "I have left her in the lounge for a while, now Tilly..." but before she could continue I had jumped up, picked up the phone that I had thrown down earlier and was dialing Mike's mobile number. Emily gently took the phone from my hand and said "Just leave it a minute."

"But I need to call Mike, I need to tell him something horrible is going on here, let me have the phone Emily or I'll just take it!" I was getting really mad and frightened and

I wasn't going to let her dictate to me, I wanted Mike, right here right now to tell me it was all going to be alright, whatever it was in that box.

Emily held fast to the phone and I gave up the struggle when I looked at her pleading face.

Five, ten I don't know just how many minutes went by before we heard the police sirens outside in the street. Emily rushed to the front door, still holding on to the phone and opened it up then came straight back into the kitchen followed closely by Toby. I jumped up at the sight of Toby "Where's Mike?" I demanded, but as I said it another policeman opened the kitchen door, looked at Toby and nodded.

"Well?" I said. "Tell me Toby, has something happened to Mike?"

With that he sat me down again and took my hand in his. "H-a-a-as he left me Toby?" All I could think of was that Mike had changed his mind and had gone off somewhere. I had not even thought about what was in the box in the hall. Then slowly, very, very slowly as I looked at the faces around me - Emily crying, Ashling crying, Toby crying

152

now, it suddenly occurred to me just what might have been
in that box.

Chapter TEN

It was twenty three weeks after the day they found Mike's head in that box.

I was still in the hospital psychiatric ward, having had a complete breakdown. They had pumped me full of tranquillisers and given me hours and hours of counselling but now they thought I was ready to face the outside world again. I, on the other hand was not quite so sure. I jumped every time I heard a strange voice, I burst into tears at the least little thing, I could still hear Mike's voice telling me everything was going to be alright but of course it wasn't. It would never be alright again, Mike wasn't going to be there any more to assure me. They had never found Mike's body, they had never found Simon, even after a massive police hunt and investigation all over not only England but overseas too, as reported sightings of the Devil came from everywhere. They drew blank after blank but Toby had assured me they were never going to give up. He had killed one of theirs and it was an unwritten law that they would find him no matter what. That of course didn't help. I had lost the man I loved more than the world but also it was because of me that his life had been taken from him. If I had never met him he would probably be happy and healthy and living a full life.

Toby had tried to convince me that it wasn't my fault but I felt totally responsible. If I had never let Simon into my life three people wouldn't be dead now. Toby explained that of course that was rubbish, he would have killed, he would have found another girl and done the same. But it didn't help, I was guilty of bringing Simon into Izzy and Mike's lives let alone that poor other girl he had killed just because she looked a bit like me. Was this horror ever going to end? I thought not. It was just a matter of time before Simon would appear again and kill who ever I was close to and then kill me!!!!

Eventually, three weeks after the doctor had told me I should go home I did. Toby, bless him, came and picked me up and took me to his new flat. He had been organising his move before the "event" as I now had been told to refer to it.

I could never have gone back to Mike's house, not ever, so Mike's parents, well his dad and step mum, who had turned out to be really wonderful people, had sorted it all out. They had got some cleaners in to completely clear and clean everything and then had put the house up for rent. I couldn't even go down the road it was in, so my brother had gone and collected my car for me and brought it to Toby's. "You can stay here for as long as you like" Toby had kindly told me but of course I knew he was only being polite. He certainly didn't want me hanging around for too long, suppose the Devil found out where I was and came after Toby too? Toby said that was nonsense but that deep down he hoped he really would go after him as they would have a better chance of capturing him if he came out into the open again. I reminded him of the way Mike had been lured into a trap by the Devil. Apparently after Mike had left me on the day of "the event" he had only got a few streets away when his car had stopped, he must have realised there was no petrol in the tank (which actually wasn't that unusual for

Mike to forget to fill up, although the police said the petrol tank had been split open). He had grabbed a petrol can from the boot (this was all on cctv) and then was seen walking towards the petrol station at the end of the road, there was no more footage of anything after about 200 metres, he had simply disappeared. No trace was ever found, not even the petrol can, it was like he was beamed up into another planet. Of course it was the Devil who did it, we all know that, but just how he can't be caught is really unbelievable. Toby said he was really clever and must have planned everything to the last letter. He must have picked Mike up in his car between the cameras, either by force although Mike was a big guy or more likely by persuasion. We will probably never know.

That first night at Toby's flat I was a bundle of nerves and had to take a couple of sleeping tablets just to calm down. Toby sat with me all night and when I eventually slept, well he still sat with me. He was snoring lightly when I woke up to find him still with one arm around me, not in a romantic way just in comfort. He woke suddenly when I moved and looked very flustered.

"Sorry Tilly" he said, "Did I wake you with my snoring?"

He was so concerned I actually smiled very slightly.

"Oh Toby, you are such a great friend. I don't know just what I would have done without you these past weeks" and with that I stood up and said I would get us some coffee.

While we sat drinking coffee I told him of my plan.

I had remembered him telling me when I was in a state in the hospital that he thought the best thing, once I felt ready of course, would be to move far away, maybe change my name, and although it sounded drastic at the time I now saw sense in it. If I stayed where I was it might only be a matter of time before the Devil would return. I know Toby was trying to make it sound very unlikely but I knew he was worried for me.

Now I had a plan. I was going to do exactly as he had suggested, break ties with all my friends and even my family, well on the surface anyway. I wouldn't tell anybody where I was living and would only contact my family by an untraceable mobile or on my computer. I would stay away for as long as it took for the police to find the bastard and lock him up forever. This was the only way I could safeguard my family and friends. I didn't think they would be in any danger once I wasn't around and I didn't think he would go after them for my whereabouts as it seems that finding me was part of his special game. Well it was a game he wasn't going to win, I convinced myself of that.

I had formed my plan over the last few days I was in the hospital, but wasn't entirely sure I would go through with it until now. I explained to Toby what I had planned, that I would go to Exeter in Devon, a place I always loved to go with my mum and dad as a child. We holidayed close to the main town there often, at a little place called Sandy Bay near Exmouth, and at one time my father had even said he would like to retire there but unfortunately he never got the chance. Well Sandy Bay was lovely but quite holiday-ish and small but Exeter was huge and I could lose myself there quite easily, or so I believed.

Mike's father and Step mum had been so wonderful about everything, considering they were grieving so much too, they gave me some money, even though I protested and said I must do what I thought was right. It was enough money for me to rent somewhere for at least a year and to live off. I was so grateful that they didn't blame me for their son's death even though I blamed myself. They said that Mike had every intention of looking after me for life so their help was just a small amount of what their son intended to do.

I knew I would need to change my name but legally I didn't really want to do that just in case it was traceable so I decided to just change my first name as it is quite legal to call yourself something different for a Christian name. As my surname was Waterson I thought I would just shorten it to Waters, that was hardly an unusual surname. The devil would be looking for a Tilly I was sure. So I decided I would be Rachel, Rachel Waters of Wolverhampton. That made Toby smile when I told him.

"But why from Wolverhampton?" he had queried.

"Dunno, it just came to me" I said in a very poor Wolverhampton accent.

I told my mother I was going to "lose" myself for while, well until they had more of an idea about the whereabouts of the Devil, she fully understood but said that I must keep in touch and my brother and Cassandra said exactly the same thing. I told them I wanted to see loads of pictures of the twins on Facebook and that I would log in regularly so we could keep in touch that way, even Skype, once this was agreed they were all a little happier with the plan. I also told my mother to keep my grandmother informed and tell her not to worry and that I would miss her and write to her often.

Within three weeks of my making the decision to move to Devon I was there. It was winter by this time and everything looked murky and grey but it didn't matter one jot to me, this was going to be a new start for me. I was just beginning to face my life again. Oh, of course I had very bad moments when all I could think about was Mike and the "event", but my counsellor had been very good at his job and had helped me no end with my morose thoughts and all my sadness. He had recommended another counsellor, a Miss Garret who had a practice on the outskirts of the city and he had passed her all my notes. I had an appointment to see her a week after I moved.

The little terraced house I was renting was lovely, warm with great central heating and cosy with a tiny fireplace with real fire in the tiny lounge. The kitchen was really homely too with everything you would need including a microwave and a real coffee machine all squashed into something tiny but very cute. My grandmother's clock, fully repaired and with the beak now painted, hung on the wall above the cooker which was inset into what was an old fireplace. It felt like a home and was going to be a great help with my recovery I was sure, or I hoped anyway. Because Mike's parents had been so generous it meant that I didn't have to go to work for a while, which was great as I didn't want to get a job and then have to leave if I got depressed again. So I thought I would maybe volunteer somewhere just in case I started to get bored. I thought I would wait until I had seen Miss Garret and then start looking for something to do.

It didn't take me long to unpack my stuff as I didn't have much with me, mainly clothes and my new computer, a few CDs , DVDs and player and a few bits of cooking equipment I really liked - and a brand new duvet and bedding. I couldn't bring myself to bring any of those from Mike's as they would hold too many memories. I was soon settled in and was sitting on the couch reading a book with the little fire crackling in the hearth when there was a knock on the front door. Panic set in immediately. "Calm, breathe. Calm, breathe," I used the exercises I had been taught. One more big breath then a quick shake of my brain to say...it is nothing. People knock on doors every day. Slowly I stood and peeped out of the front window. Standing at my door was a lady in a thick coat with a huge scarf wrapped around her neck looking very cold. I tapped on the window and motioned that I was on my way and she smiled. A warm smile which made my nerves instantly disappear. I opened the front door and secretly hoped she wasn't a Jehovah's Witness.

"Rachel Waters?" she asked as I came face to face with her, and as I nodded continued "Sorry, I don't mean to bother you if you are busy, but I work at the letting agents and as I didn't get a chance to meet you when you picked up the keys to this place I thought I would come and introduce myself. I am Lucy, Lucy Miller." She held out her hand then realised she had big furry gloves on and pulled her hand back then pulling off the glove she held her hand out again. We both smiled and I realised I hadn't even invited her in and it was freezing outside. I immediately remedied that and she gratefully accepted my invitation to come into the lounge.

"Please" I said "take a seat, can I get you some tea or coffee?"

"Well that would be lovely if it is not too much trouble" she said. "I don't want to disturb you if you're busy."

I made the coffee and opened a packet of ginger nuts, then proceeded to put a piece of kitchen roll on a plate before putting the biscuits out....then realising I was turning into my mother I quickly took the kitchen roll off!

We sat opposite each other with a little coffee table in between. Lucy started the conversation with "I hope the house is OK for you, I understand from the office that you have only just moved into this area." Obviously there was nothing wrong in this statement but shivers started to go down my spine.

"Why is she asking me questions?...don't be so stupid" I told myself, "Of course she is going to ask questions." I explained that I felt my life wasn't on the right track, I had been in a relationship but wasn't anymore and I thought a new challenge would be good for me. As I had holidayed near Exeter when I was a child I thought I would give it a go down here. This seemed to satisfy her, maybe she wasn't even interested but was just being polite. Well after about half an hour of chit chat and once we had finished our coffee I expected her to get up to go but she didn't.

"Was there anything you wanted other than to check if I like the house?" I said.

"Not really" she replied, "but to be totally honest it is so cold out there and I am so cosy sitting here I was just hanging on a bit!" This statement totally broke the ice and we both started to laugh. I stood up, went to the kitchen and returned with two glasses and a bottle of wine, her face was a picture when I walked back in.

"Er, if it's not too early?" I gestured towards the bottle.

"Never!" Lucy replied and the friendship was cemented.

Chapter ELEVEN

I was so glad that Lucy had knocked on my door that night. We became firm friends and were soon going out to movies, wine bars, pubs etc together. Lucy introduced me to several of her other friends and we soon became a sort of small crowd, going to gigs together, to see the local bands and sometimes some bigger bands in Torquay and around. Calling each other up to let each of us know just what was going on around town etc. It was like a new life for me...well it WAS a new life for me! I was actually having fun, which is something I never thought I would ever do again.

The summer came and went and suddenly I realised it was winter again and I had been in Exeter for more than a year. I had been keeping in touch with my family via Skype and Tom had visited me with Cassandra and the twins, even Toby had been down on a couple of occasions and brought my mother on one such trip. Of course I missed my family and the twins growing up but I felt safe and content down here in Devon. There had been no sightings or anything with regard to Simon's whereabouts but that didn't mean they had stopped looking, Toby had assured me.

Well the winter left us almost as soon as it had arrived that year, whether it was because my life was fuller again or whether it was actually a really short one but, hey, it was spring before I realised it.

I had been volunteering at the local hospital for about six months, taking people to and fro for hospital visits and sometimes in the building itself fetching books or items from the shop for patients who were stuck in their beds. Getting new mothers, who had to stay put due to premature babies or such, magazines or disposable nappies. I loved doing all this, but the time had come for me to get a proper job where I earned money. The money that Mike's parents had given me had almost run out, although they had kindly offered to give me some more I had refused, as I didn't think it was their job to keep me. I had, though, promised to keep in touch with them and let them know if I needed anything.

My savings were going to have to come into play now with the bills almost due, but they weren't going to last long. Several times I went to the local job centre but there was nothing that was remotely good for me and I was beginning to feel a little down. It was after one of these visits that I went to the wine bar that we, as a crowd, used in the centre of town and ordered a half carafe of red wine and a cheese salad club sandwich. I sat looking into my half empty wine glass feeling sorry for myself when I heard a loud voice saying "Drowning your sorrows, eh? And in the middle of the day too!"

I turned smartly to look behind me and saw Karen, one of the friends I had made with Lucy, standing behind me with a child of about eighteen months or so in her arms. Smiling, I pointed to the seat opposite me and she dragged the pushchair that was behind her and placed the now sleeping child into it.

"I didn't know you were a mum" I said. Karen had never mentioned any family of her own and was always out with us.

"And I didn't know you were a secret drinker," she said, then added "Mine? Nah, this is my sister's youngest, she had to go to the dentist with her boy so I said I would hold onto this little one for an hour or so. And look, good old auntie Karen gives her a cuddle and she falls asleep. Story of my life, eh!" We both laughed at her joke. Karen was not one to worry about who knew what about her activities. "If I fancy a bloke and want to go to bed with him, who is to tell me I can't eh?" she was always saying, "Life's too short to worry about what people think of you."

Minutes later the waitress arrived with my sandwich and seeing Karen eye it longingly I ordered another and another glass. We shared the first sandwich and a glass of wine each then when the second one arrived we shared that too and a second glass of wine. I was feeling so much better after an hour with Karen, she had a way of being funny even if a bit course at times but was a really nice person under all her bravado. I asked her why she thought she had never met the right man, well so far, or was she just out for fun and no commitment? She laughed and replied that she would love to meet the right man but there probably wasn't a man alive who could control her.

"What about you" she suddenly said " You never talk about your past, did you have a bloke and it went wrong? Oh, sorry. You're not gay are you? I mean it doesn't matter a jot to me if you are."

I was really tempted to tell her everything, due probably to the amount of wine in me but I managed to stop myself and just said "No I'm not gay and I did have a relationship but not anymore." Karen was astute enough not to push me, as I think she could see the odd tear appearing in my eyes and so dropped the subject.

The baby suddenly decided to wake up and so Karen shot off to take her home.

"See you in the pub on Friday!" she called as she left and I just did a thumbs up sign and poured the last of the wine into my glass.

Friday arrived and we all met in the pub for our usual drinks and decisions on what we were going to do for the next seven days. Lilly, one of the girls, suggested we went to see the new James Bond movie. This sent the famous shivers down my spine so I asked, "Is there another new one, It seems only a short time since the last one was out."

"Wow, that was three years ago!" they all echoed then I realised, three years ago since I met the Devil that night and he showed the first signs of his madness and I didn't pick up on it. If I had nobody would be dead now, and if and if......the thoughts started to buzz around my head like a tornado, what if, what if...................

The next thing I knew I was laying on a sofa in the back room of the pub. The land lady Paula was sitting next to me with bowl and a cloth.

"Are you feeling any better?" she asked. "I think you might have had a little too much to drink deary, do you feel sick?" She lifted the bowl but I shook my head.

"I am so sorry, what happened?" I said,

"Well you just keeled over and fell off your chair so your friends asked if you could come in here for a lie down." she

171

said. "Would you like some black coffee or a drink of water or something?"

"I'm not drunk" I protested. "I have only had a half of cider."

"I hope you're not saying it was our cider" her attitude suddenly went on the defensive, for which I couldn't blame her really.

"No, no, of course not" I replied. "I just had something on my mind and things we were talking about suddenly brought it to the surface and I fainted. I am so very sorry to put you to this trouble" and with that I tried to get up but she pushed me back down and said, very gently this time "Would you like me to get a doctor to take a look at you, you don't just faint for nothing. You're not pregnant or anything are you?" she meant it kindly and was trying to help but this didn't help, my head started to swim again.

I have to get out of here I told myself. I took some deep breaths. Calm, breathe, calm breathe, remember what the doctor told you. Within a few minutes I felt a little better and pulled myself up.

"I feel fine now" I said to Paula, "Again I am sorry if I caused you any trouble, I'm not pregnant and I don't need a doctor, give me another cider and I will be just fine" I tried to look natural and must have succeeded as she smiled and followed me out to the bar where the "crowd" were all sitting.

"Aah! The wanderer returns!" they chorused, then seeming more concerned than the others Lucy grabbed my hand.

"Are you sure you are OK Rachel? You gave us quite a scare, had you been drinking before you came down here tonight?"

I realised that they all obviously thought I was drunk but I couldn't be bothered to explain so just said no but that I had had something for lunch that maybe didn't agree with me. They all seemed satisfied with my explanation and Paula arrived with my cider and so the evening continued, luckily with no more mention of the James Bond movie, they had all forgotten about that.

The next day we had all decided to go bowling. It wasn't the sort of thing we did very often but there were no bands playing locally and nobody had mentioned the cinema again, so bowling it was. We were all to meet at the Mecca Bowls in the city at 7.30pm. Lucy said she would pick me up as I was closer to the Mecca than her, so when 7.50pm arrived and she hadn't showed I started to wonder if she had forgotten me. I called her mobile but just got a voice mail, very unusual for Lucy not to show up or at least tell me to find my own way. Still as I say, I thought maybe she had forgotten so I made my own way there on foot - it was only about half an hour's walk. When I arrived the gang were all set up and had started their first games. There was no sign of Lucy though and none of the guys had seen or heard anything from her. I tried her mobile again but again got voice mail, so I left a second message just saying I was worried and hoped that everything was OK. Karen and I paired up for a game against Lilly and Josh, but my mind was still on Lucy. We won our game easily and went to the bar to get more drinks, and then Lucy arrived, looking very sheepish and apologetic.

"I'm so sorry Rach" she said, "I was on my way, honestly, but at the end of my road there was this guy who had broken down so I stopped and helped him push his car to the side of the road and then he said he wanted to thank me by taking me for a drink while he waited for the breakdown truck to show up...well he was very persuasive and really cute so I stayed and had a drink with him, are you really angry?"

"Of course not, you idiot" I said. "I was just worried that something had happened to you. Come on then tell us all about the mystery guy, are you going to see him again?"

"Well he took my number, so he might just call you never know!" I gave her a hug and said I was delighted for her, he could be the man of her dreams, I said. We all patted her on the back and made kissy kissy noises until she told us all to just shut up. But she was smiling when she said it.

When we had all played our games everyone decided to go on to the pub but Lucy and I decided to call it a night as she had to be up bright and early in the morning to run some errands and I was tired anyway. We got back to my place and Lucy came in for a coffee.

"Come on then," I said when we were sitting at the kitchen table with our coffees. "Tell me all, what is his name, what does he look like?"

"Well" she said "His name is Mike (the normal shiver I was beginning to get used to shot down my spine as usual when any reference connected to my past was mentioned, no matter how distant. Calm, breathe ,calm ...)

"Great!" was all I could come up with, and "That's a nice name, Mike."

"Well yes," she said "he really was very nice - and charming even. He asked me all about myself, what I did for a living, where I went when I went out, who my friends were, how long I had lived in Exeter"

"Wow!" I said, "Was he from the Spanish inquisition?"

She looked a little hurt. "No he was just showing an interest I'm sure."

"Sorry" I said. "Maybe he is a detective and is just used to asking a lot of questions." At this statement Lucy laughed. "Well actually, he is..."

"What?" I said " a detective?"

"Yes he is, he's with the CID in Southampton, Hampshire but he's down here on a course."

"Oh sorry Luce" I said, "there might not be a lot of chance of him being your Prince Charming if he lives miles away."

"Well that is just it" she said."He likes it down here so much he is thinking of putting in for a transfer, or so he said anyway, but he might just have been saying that so I would think he would be in touch I suppose, but Rach he was really really nice and so good looking." We finished out coffee and Lucy went on her way. I locked all the doors and windows and started to head off to bed when my mobile rang. It was Toby

"How's it going Till..er sorry Rachel ?" I tried calling you hours ago so I assume you were out having a ball"

"Oh yes. Sorry Toby" I said "We were all at the bowling alley so I switched off my phone while we were playing. Is everything alright? I mean is this a social call or has something happened, my mum's OK isn't she?" I started to panic when he didn't reply straight away. "Toby, tell me, is there something wrong with my mum?"

"No, No, nothing like that, your mum is fine and Tom and the family. It's just...well we think there may have been a sighting of Simon, we are not totally sure as the person who saw him didn't get a really long look at him, but as he is one of our officers and he thinks it was Simon I trust him enough to start the hunt again"

I was numb. "Where and when was he spotted?" I asked Toby, the usual shiver building in my spine like a volcano erupting very slowly.

"Well, our source says he was in Basingstoke on Tuesday and saw a car that appeared to be broken down at the side of the road just before the M3 junction so he stopped to ask if the driver needed any help. But he said the driver was quite evasive, kept his hand over his mouth when he spoke, said he had a cold and didn't want to pass on any germs. He said help was on its way. Well once the PC was sure he didn't need any more help he went on his way. As he drove off he started to think he had seen the man before. He said he had the beginnings of a beard but he was sure he had seen his face unshaven somewhere.

When he got back to the station in Guildford he started to look though mug shots and found Simon....he's pretty sure it was him but obviously now sporting a beard. Now don't get worried Till.. er Rachel, this was in Basingstoke. Miles away from where you are and I really don't think there is any chance he will find you, but I felt I should let you know."

My heart had sunk at his words as I had convinced myself that the Devil was now living abroad somewhere but I suppose deep down I knew he would try and get to me, after all he was bloody crazy.

I didn't sleep too well that night, well that is if I slept at all. When the alarm clock went off in the morning it felt like I hadn't slept for days so I must have dropped off for a while. I had a rotten Sunday, just moping around the house feeling sorry for myself and watching rubbish TV. Lucy called and said she would come round but I didn't much feel like talking to anybody so I put her off. By 8.00pm I was feeling really tired so I went off to bed with a book and slept until the alarm woke me the next morning.

 I was in the kitchen brewing some coffee when the front door knocker made me almost jump out of my skin. I peeped through the living room curtains to see Karen standing at the door, or rather lounging with one foot back against the wall and a cigarette in her hand. Relieved I opened the door, after releasing a dead bolt and two other locks and a chain.

"Wow!" Karen commented as she threw the remains of her cigarette into one of my plant pots, then seeing my face picked it back out and squashed it against the wall and then put it in her pocket "Your house is like Fort Knox....who are you afraid of?"

I didn't reply, just waved my hand for her to come in.

"I've come to do you a favour" she started with "Are you still looking for a job?" I nodded, so she continued "Well I know you are an office bod, but if you fancy doing something very different there is an opening at the dog grooming salon where I work." She quickly continued when she saw the horrified look on my face. "Nah not grooming the dogs! On reception. You could learn to groom as well of course if you fancied it" she added with a twinkle in her eye. Trust Karen to come up with something for me just when I thought I was never going to find work.

"Well" I said, "I'd love to come and see the owner and see if I would be any good."

At this she laughed and shrugged. "Actually I am the owner" she said " and you would be perfect!".

I had no idea that Karen was so, er, what would I call her – intelligent? Nah - professional? Nah. Well I just didn't think she was clever enough. No that's not it. Oh, I don't know, but she doesn't seem the type that would actually have the savvy to open, own and make a success of a business. Well done to you I thought.

"Well if I have the job then Karen, when can I start?Oh and of course how much can I earn?" With this she delved into her huge bag lady type carpet bag and dragged out a folder.

"Here ya go" she handed it to me. "Shall I pour that coffee that's sitting there while you have a read through? If it was later in the day I would suggest we have a glass of something instead but it is only 9.00am and even I am not that bad".

We agreed that I would start the following Monday. Once Karen had left I felt really exhilarated. I cleaned the house from top to bottom, which didn't take long as it was very small then I called Lucy to ask her if she fancied coming out for some lunch if she could get away. The one thing about

181

working for a rental agency means you can take your lunch whenever you feel like it, or so she had told me anyway. "Oh I would have loved to Rach" she said "but you will never guess what, that policeman I met yesterday called me up and invited me out for lunch, in fact I can see him out of my window leaning against his car waiting"

"Oh" I said "you had better get going. But you must come round tonight and tell me all about it."

She readily agreed, said she would bring the wine and that was that. I sat for a moment twiddling my fingers then thought - retail therapy, that's what I need, and something new to wear on Monday.

I bought two new skirts, a pair of jeans and a gorgeous white fluffy jumper. I was so pleased with my purchases that I popped into the wine bar on my way home and ordered a half carafe of red wine to celebrate, even if I was on my own I could still celebrate I thought. Well almost experiencing déjà vu a voice rang out behind me.

"Drinking alone, eh? So this is what you get up to on a Monday afternoon."

It wasn't Karen this time but Lilly. She did exactly the same thing as Karen had done that time I had met her in exactly this same wine bar and in exactly this same seat. She pulled up a chair opposite me and beckoned the waitress for a second glass and ordered another carafe of wine.

"Can't have you drinking alone now can we?" she smiled and poured her wine. "So what brings you out here all alone" she continued.

"I could say the same to you" I replied smiling.

"Touché!" she said. "Actually I was walking past on my way home when I saw you sitting here all alone." At this she suddenly started to look around, "Er, you are alone aren't you?" then realising that I only had one glass in front of me she laughed. "Sorry, that was a stupid thing to say, you are obviously on your own or whoever you are with doesn't drink!" That made her laugh again.

"Well actually" I replied, "Back at you! I am celebrating! I have a job and I start next Monday!"

"Oh great! So Karen persuaded you to join her little empire then, I am so glad!"

"Oh, have you been discussing me then?" I was a little hurt but decided not to say anything.

"No, nothing like you think" she said. "It was just Karen was saying that her receptionist had handed in her notice and she didn't know what she was going to do as getting somebody reliable was really difficult. It was as she said this that we had both said at the same time – Rachel!"

I felt a lot better then, the thought that had run through my mind before was that they all felt sorry for me and thought maybe the episode in the pub on Friday night might just have been that I had been drinking before I had gone out. "Fancy something to eat?" I asked. "We could have lunch to help this wine go down."

We sat there and had some good laughs about all the gang and time simply disappeared. Lilly told me that she was secretly in love with Tristan, one of the guys we all knocked about with, but that he had never really shown any interest in her. We tried to think of ways she could encourage him without actually telling him that she fancied him like crazy. Once we got on this subject we ordered more wine and laughed more and more but never really came to any sensible conclusion.

It was half past four when we left the wine bar, a little drunk, and headed back to my house for either more wine or coffee, we hadn't decided which.

Once back at my place we sensibly settled on some coffee and had some biscuits before Lilly left. I was expecting Lucy to come round later so thought I would make a curry for us to enjoy. Well "later with Lucy" didn't arrive, because she called and cancelled. She said she had had such a wonderful lunch with Mike it had spilled over into the afternoon then they had decided to go out for dinner in the evening. She hoped I would understand, which of course I did. I was happy for her, I just hoped she wasn't going to get herself all keen on him and then him go back to Southampton or wherever he came from, and leave her in the lurch. I took the curry out of the oven but didn't really feel like eating, I just thought I would have a soak in the tub and an early night with my book. I was just running the water when the phone rang. It was Toby.

"I just thought I would let you know that we haven't got any further with our search."

I thanked him but just before I hung up something made me ask "Toby, what kind of car was he driving... this man your officer thought might be Simon?"

"Oh it wasn't the green one he had before, it was a silver BMW, not very new", then added at that remark "Well it wouldn't be, if it had broken down, now would it? He hung up after promising me he would call me if there was any news.

After I hung up I went to the front door and checked I had the dead bolt on and the chain and the double lock, then checked the back door and did the same, then all the windows. "Am I getting paranoid again?" I thought. "No, just being sensible", then I had a wonderful soak in the bath and went to bed.

The rest of the week flew by with very little happening. On Tuesday I Skyp'ed my mum and we had a lovely long chat. She had met a man she told me, his name was Anthony pronounced with the TH sound not just the T. He had been at one of the quiz evenings that she had started going to with her Chelsea Flower Show friends. They were held at her local pub and apparently AnTHony was one of the ladies' brothers. Recently divorced, he was staying with Angie, his sister, for a couple of weeks. Well my mum said he was really nice, they had talked about films that they would like to see and so he had taken her to the pictures AND they had eaten fish and chips out of the paper on the way home. For some reason this made me smile, thinking of my mum strolling along eating not only in a public street but out of paper and without a doily! I was very happy for her of course and told her so. "Now don't start making wedding plans for me just yet" she said.

Then on Wednesday I Skyp'ed my brother and Cassandra pulled the twins over to the camera so they could say "Night, Night!" to auntie Tilly. It broke my heart not being able to give them a cuddle but Tom promised they would visit in a week or so.

The rest of the week was very quiet. I didn't see the crowd as most of them were off doing their own stuff that weekend and Karen must have been busy with her new man as I didn't see or hear anything from her.

Monday arrived very quickly though and I was quite excited at the prospect of working again, even if it was just as a receptionist. Karen's dog grooming business was really something else. There was a nice clean and modern reception, you could almost mistake it for a doctor or dentist surgery except for the lovely pictures of "before and after" dogs all over the walls. I had a computer to log all the visits. There were four groomers working full time and two trainees doing the bathing of the dogs. The rooms were at the back where the grooming was done. Each dog had a record card with a picture of each visit, both before and after so that if the owner wanted the same clip or something different the groomer would know what was done before. In fact it was run almost like posh hair stylist salon really. Karen certainly had her head on straight for this business. The place was booked weeks in advance. She also had a small outlet for doggie extras such as leads, collars and treats. I knew instantly I was really going to enjoy working here.

I got into the swing of things almost at once. Karen came in to see how I was getting on, she didn't actually work in the salon herself, although fully trained she said she had done it for years and now as it was so successful she was going to take a back seat. Maybe she would open another salon in a different town, but not till after she had a year or two off. She would always jump in if somebody was off sick but she liked just popping in to check on things, and then have the rest of her time for herself. None of us knew what 'time for herself' actually meant as she never told anybody just what she was up to, but that was her prerogative.

I hadn't heard from Lucy for almost a week when I bumped into her in town while I was getting a sandwich.

"Oh, Hi Rach!" she greeted me, with a huge smile on her face "Listen before you get cross with me, I have news"

"I'm not cross with you" I had started to say but she shhhhed me.

"Mike and I are going out properly together and I might even ask him to move in" she gabbled. "He is going to relocate down here and Oh Rach I think I really love him"

"But it's only been a couple of weeks" I tried to say but she carried on babbling.

"I know you'll think it's much too soon but Rach when you know it's right it just is, please say you are happy for me"

"Of course I am" I said and put one arm around her "If you say it's right then it is fine by me, and of course I am happy for you. So when can we meet this Mr Right then?"

She stopped babbling then and went quiet.

"Well", she said "It's not that he is shy or anything but he feels we should be really more sure of each other before we start mixing with each other's friends, so if you don't mind we will wait just a little while".

Very slight alarm bells went off in my head as she said this, maybe because I had heard it said to me before or maybe I just thought he must be a bit of a selfish bloke not to want to be involved with her life. It's not as if she could be involved in his as all his friends probably lived miles away. It seemed to me that he was a bit of a control freak if he didn't want to share her with her friends. Shit....something suddenly started to take a bit of shape in my stupid head.

"No don't be daft" I told myself, "It can't be."

"Let's go and get a quick coffee and we can catch up" I said brightly

"OK" she said, "but I can't be long. I am meeting Mike in half an hour and he hates it when I am late"...again nasty little niggles started to form and my spine started its tingling again.

Over coffee she told me all about how Mike did this and Mike said that. How he wanted to hear all about her friends, especially Lilly. Unusual name that, apparently he had said, don't get many Lillie's to the pound he had joked and Lucy thought it funny.

"Is it short for anything?" he had asked.

All this babble coming out of Lucy's mouth and all I could think of was "the Devil".

Just as we were parting company, Lucy in a bit of a flap as she thought she was late, I suddenly said "What car has Mike got then Lucy?"

"Oh some old BMW" she said. "Nice old thing, breaks down a lot though apparently!"

"What colour?" I asked.

"Why?" she said. "Does the colour have anything to do with it breaking down?" she smiled.

"No of course not" I said "I was just curious."

"Oh you!" she said, kissed my cheek and was gone.

I went back to work and tried to concentrate but all I could think of was why was he asking questions about Lilly in particular and it's the same type of car that Toby had told me about....I just couldn't get it out of my mind but after a few calls from customers and a few pats of well groomed dogs, by the time I went home I had decided it was all in my mind and I was being stupid.

I was sure Mike was a good guy. Lucy wasn't daft and so what if he was a bit of a control freak, they weren't all like Simon.

Chapter TWELVE

Well a few weeks went by and I heard nothing from Lucy. She had dropped off our crowd scene completely. I didn't worry as I thought that if she was unhappy she would be in touch and I didn't like to phone her as I thought she might think I was jealous of her having a boyfriend and try to meddle. The rest of the gang didn't seem to bother, they said they were used to members dropping in and out of the crowd when boyfriends or girlfriends took preference. They would either return or we would get invites to their weddings. If I went anywhere without the crowd it was usually with Karen as she seemed to always be around when there was a girlie movie on somewhere or I just fancied a pizza out. We got on really well even though she was technically my boss and paid my wages - she was still just a friend as she was rarely in the salon these days.

It was on one of these pizza nights that we chatting and both of us remarked that we hadn't actually seen Lucy, or for that matter Lilly, for ages and that we should really arrange a girlie night out very soon. We were literally working out a date when suddenly Tristan came rushing into the pizza bar.

"Have you heard?" he said, "Lilly has been attacked!"

"What?" we both said at the same time, jumping up from our seats.

"When, where"? I said.

"It happened last night" Tristan said, sitting down at our table and motioning us to do the same. "She is in All Saints Hospital and in quite a bad way...she apparently was hit from behind and then after she fell she was punched in the face really badly. They don't know why as her purse was still intact and they haven't a clue as to who or why. I only just found out myself, as the police were hoping to keep it under wraps until they had something to go on just in case he attacked again...

"Or she" I added" although I have no idea why I said that.

"Yes of course" Tristan agreed. My pulse was racing and my spine was heading for complete electric overload.

194

"Can we go and see her?" I asked him, but he said they weren't letting any visitors in at the moment and that she had a policeman sitting with her so that when, or if, she woke up he could get a statement.

"What do you mean "If"? Tristan, do they think she might not?"

Tristan shrugged and I could see tears beginning to erupt in his eyes. Maybe he is sweet on her I thought, or maybe he's just sorry as she is one of the gang. I did think that when she gets better, and I hoped so much that she would, that she should or I would tell him how she feels about him. But now was not the time.

I said goodbye to Karen as soon as I could comfortably do so and rushed home, checking and re-checking all my doors and windows once I was inside. I poured myself a brandy and picking up the phone I dialled Toby's mobile.

He picked up after the second ring. I was crying by the time I had finished telling him all about Lilly but he was very calm and said he would look into it and come down at the weekend and go through my concerns with me. He said it

195

was unlikely that Simon was involved but to re assure me we could go though it together. I had told him about Lucy and Mike and the car but he had said there loads of old BMW's about, so I was not to get paranoid. I sensed he was a little fed up with my paranoia or that it was just in my head !!!!

It was the weekend and Toby arrived Saturday morning at just after 10am. I had been up for what seemed like hours fidgeting around and wondering what Toby would say. I had convinced myself that the person who attacked Lilly was Simon, I have no real idea why I should think that, other than piecing together everything Lucy had told me and adding it all up to make, what, I didn't know ten, twenty, One!!!.

As soon as Toby arrived he suggested we go out for breakfast which we did.

"Right", he started with once we had sat down in Costa's with croissants and huge coffees "I had a word with the police investigating Lilly's attack but they have no leads as yet. Apparently she had just got off the bus at Lloyd street and was walking towards the Galleries shopping centre at 4.17pm, that much they have traced on cameras, but then for no apparent reason she stopped and started to walk in a different direction down towards the old mill - you know it?" I nodded and he continued "Now they think she might have seen something or her phone might have rung, as she seemed to look in her bag but then disappeared from view as the bloody cameras don't go down that far.   That is everything they have. The first they knew about it was at 7.00pm, when a woman walking her dog saw what she thought was a bag of clothes dumped on the ground near the wall just before the mill entrance. Her dog had gone over to it and was barking so she followed, which was lucky or Lilly may not have been found until much later and probably wouldn't be alive now. She is still unconscious by the way, but they think there has been a little improvement"

I nodded again that I knew this as I had called the hospital several times to check up on her condition.

"Well that is probably as much as I know and probably as much as you know then isn't it"?

"Well not quite" I said " I have a real strong feeling that this is the work of Simon."

"Oh now Till....Rachel" Toby started, "You can't put everything down to him. I know he is capable but if we follow those lines all the time we might be looking in the wrong direction and the real attacker might be right under their noses, get away, or even worse attack again."

"OK, OK, I get all that" I said "but Toby - I spoke to Lucy the other day and she was telling me about her new boyfriend, whose name happens to be Mike and who happens to be a policeman. Don't you think that is a bit of a coincidence? Also who happens to have asked a lot of questions about Lilly and who owns a BMW? Toby I am convinced it is him"

 I took a huge slug of coffee and waited for him to reply. He didn't. He just looked thoughtful for a while, nibbled on a croissant then put his hand over mine.

"I know what you, what we all went though sweetheart but you can't think everything that happens is Simon. There are such things as coincidences after all. This guy, this Mike,

Lucy's boyfriend, can't we just go and see him and then we will know"

I know he was humouring me but it seemed a perfect idea, why hadn't I just barged around to Lucy's house and insisted on meeting this Mike?

"Ok" I said, "let's do that! If we meet him I will know it's just in my head, if we don't then will you at least check it out for me? After all he is supposed to be with the force in Southampton."

With that Toby picked up my hand and shook it, "Deal!" he said and took a huge bite of his croissant.

I felt so much better after breakfast with Toby. He left me in the cafe and said he would go to the police station and see if he could trace this Mike, and in turn I would call Lucy and arrange to go visit. Surely she couldn't turn me down if I said I was bringing my, as I would pretend to her, boyfriend Toby, who is also a copper? I finished my coffee and got out my phone but before I had a chance to use it a call came in...it was Lucy.

"Wow this is uncanny" I said once I had answered it. "I was just about to call you!"

"Rachel!" she sobbed into the phone. "Can you come round? I really need to talk to you!"

"I'll be there in ten" I said, then sending a quick text to Toby and advising him of her address I shot out of the door and jumped into a cab.

Lucy opened the door as soon as she heard the taxi pull up. She looked terrible, black eye make-up smeared around her eye like she had been crying, then I noticed a huge bruise on her forehead. As soon as I got inside she hugged me.

"Oh Rach, he's gone!" she said. I pulled her back and pointed to her head.

"How did you get that bruise?" was all I could think of to say to her , my thoughts flying towards Simon again, my god it must be him I thought. We went into her tiny kitchen and sat down. "Well?" I wanted to know. "The bruise?" and pointing to it said "Where did you get it? Come on, Lucy."

Then I noticed some other marks on her neck, like finger marks. "And those?" She looked so sad my heart went out to her, but my anger at the bastard was so strong that I couldn't resist staring at her again and shouting this time. "Where did you get those marks Lucy?"

She sat twiddling a tissue and began with "He left me Rachel, just like that!"

"Yes but those marks, tell me please Lucy. It is really important."

"He didn't mean to hurt me," she wailed, "he would only get upset if I was late or didn't do what he wanted. He was going to get some treatment."

With this last statement I grabbed her and hugged her, "Oh Lucy, thank goodness he's gone!....thank goodness you are still alive! Oh my God! Oh my God!" I kept saying.

Lucy pulled away and just stared at me as if I had gone mad.   But I knew without a doubt now that this was the work of the Devil.

Toby arrived soon after Lucy had told me everything. She kept saying that when "Mike" (as we decided to still call him that for the moment as Lucy was still convinced it wasn't the guy I'd told her he was) was nice he was very, very, nice but when he got mad he just lashed out.

A bit like the rhyme I thought, about the girl who when she was good she was very, very, good but when she was bad she was horrid! Stupid how things like that pop into your mind when they have no reason on earth to be there, especially at time like this - maybe it's a release valve.

Lucy said that at first "Mike" was very charming and kind. He was very genteel with her, after a few dates they had taken it a little further and ended up in bed together. That was the first time he had shown any type of anger. He had asked her to do something she didn't feel happy doing - she refused to tell me what exactly but I had a really good idea as he had tried to get me to do the same. She said when she said she didn't want to, he just got mad and got astride her, then put his hands around her throat! She said she thought he was just play acting at first but then he tightened his hands until she cried for him to stop.

Then as suddenly as he had gripped her he stopped and said it was all a joke. She said she had believed him at the time but after a few slaps, or actual punches later in their relationship she thought that maybe he hadn't been playing that day. Although she said he always said how sorry he was and that he didn't know why he behaved in that way. He was going to get treatment, he had promised.

I had listened quietly to this repeat of my previous life with him. I let her cry, I let her sob it out. She still ended up saying she would have him back as she didn't think he was really that bad. That was when Toby arrived. We sat with her, together each holding one of her hands and carefully explained everything we knew. By the time we had finished and Lucy had told Toby everything she had told me, he too was convinced that it was Simon.

Lucy was shaking once we had told her just what Simon (or in her head Mike), was capable of.

"You mean he would probably have killed me?" we nodded. "Oh my God, was it him who attacked Lilly? Do you think he might have thought she was you, Rachel? But why?"

It was then that we told her everything about me changing my name and how he had the name Tilly in his head. We will never know for sure whether he just thought I might have changed just the first letter of my name or whether it was just because it sounded the same but either way we are pretty sure he was responsible for the attack on Lilly.

Finally Toby asked Lucy what colour was Mike's car and as soon as she said Silver he grabbed his phone and went out into the hall to the station leaving Lucy and me hugging. She was still crying but more with relief I think now.

Toby returned a few minutes later.

"I'm sorry I didn't trust what you said before Tilly" he said, "it was just that so much had happened and it is all too easy to jump to conclusions. I'm sure now and we will get him. Now ladies" he said, " we are going to take you to a house where you will be safe from him should he come back."

"But he found me, Toby" I said "how did he do that for God's sake, I took all the precautions to be untraceable. What makes you think I will ever be safe from him, even in a safe house, unless he's behind bars? And now on top of it all I have brought all this trouble with me. Poor Lilly, lying in the hospital and we don't even know if she will pull though. And Lucy here - he would never have been here if I hadn't come down here."

Lucy put her arm around me and said it couldn't all be my fault. Then it suddenly dawned on me, why did he leave

Lucy?...why did he just up and go without hurting her anymore, obviously I was so relieved that he did, but why? He must have fled because of Lilly but he didn't know anybody was on to him so he could have come back here. "What happened?" I asked Lucy. "Exactly how did he just go?"

She explained that she had been asked to work late and so had phoned the local police station, where he said he was taking a course, and asked to speak with him or maybe leave a message for him. He had told her she must never call him at work but she knew how angry he got if she was late so she thought on this occasion he wouldn't mind. When they said they had never heard of him she panicked and thought maybe he had asked them to say that. Maybe he wanted to end it, but didn't want to tell her so thought he'd just ignore her, after all that's what guys did wasn't it, she had had experience of this. Well, she thought, I'm not having that. So she left a message on his mobile telling him exactly that, that she had phoned his work and that they had said they had never heard of him, she said she deserved better so was going to phone the station in Southampton and tell his colleagues just what a coward he was.

This must have been the trigger to make him take flight, in case she found out he was never employed there, or maybe realised he wasn't even a policeman.

Well whatever the reason she had had a very lucky escape. Toby said. Lucy must get some things together to take to the safe house and while she did he would take me back to mine to do the same. My spine hadn't stopped tingling since I arrived at Lucy's and realised my fears were not unfounded. I didn't want to run from the Devil but I really did feel it was the right thing to do, knowing just what he was capable of.

"There is a guard at the hospital with Lilly isn't there?" I asked Toby. "I mean, if he thinks she is still alive he might try and get to her so she won't be able to identify him."

"I doubt he needs to worry about that" Toby replied. "For one thing he grabbed her from behind and then punched her so severely in her face I am sure she wouldn't have seen his face anyway. Also I don't think he would even care as I expect he knows by now that we know it was him. He will do his disappearing act again but we have a little more to go on this time and I have no doubt we will get him soon"

I packed a case and collected everything I would need for a week or so. I wondered if both Lucy and I would be safe going to work. Toby said he would feel happier if we made sure we were never on our own going to and from work. Once we got to the house we decided that Lucy would drop me off at work then drive on to her work which was only about five minutes away, and that if she was worried at all she would drive straight to the police station, then we would do the reverse at the end of the day. We would only go out of the house together, never alone. Although Toby said he thought Simon would be in hiding now anyway for a while at least, until he formed his next plan. Mind you this didn't give us a lot of comfort.

Well we settled in to the house, which turned out to be really nice. Toby had stopped at the supermarket on our way and waited outside while we shopped for provisions including a few bottles of wine, a bottle of gin, a bottle of brandy and two of Prosecco.

"Wow!" he had said."It's like being back at Uni! did you actually get any food as well?"

Once he had gone we double locked all the doors. He had told us there would be a drive by patrol car every two hours or so just checking everything was clear and that if we had any anxieties we could call him or just dial 999. There were emergency buttons fitted in several rooms in the house which were directly linked to the police. Lucy had calmed down and was now just feeling relieved instead of her original hurt. She wanted to know why I had kept it all a secret from her and the rest of the gang and I tried to explain that it was supposed to be a new start for me, I had no idea he would find me and still had no clue as to how he did.

"Let's drop the subject for a while shall we?" she eventually said. "Get the glasses out and let's get as pissed as possible, I certainly feel like it."

"We had better have something to eat first" I said "I'll make us some supper and you can be the barman."

Life took a turn for the better again for the next few weeks, Lucy and I were still in the safe house. There had been no sightings of Simon. Lilly had started to recover but was still in the hospital and still very weak. We visited her often to try and cheer her up, we even bought her a stupid wig which made her laugh for the first time in ages. While she was in intensive care they had taken her to theatre and shaved a side of her head so they could operate to relieve some of the pressure the beating had caused. She said she wouldn't leave the hospital until it had grown back. So we bought the wig and sent Tristan in with it which cheered her up, especially when he asked her if she would go out with him when she was discharged. We had all piled in after Tris and when she laughed we all clapped loudly, until a nurse came in and shooed us all out saying we were disturbing the other patients.

Toby had been around several times, although he had gone back to his base in Guildford and it was a long way for him to keep coming. I kept telling him we were fine but he came anyway, and in a way I was glad, I felt much safer when he was around. Lucy and I were such good mates now. Well we were told to go everywhere together to be safe but I really think we actually wanted to.

After five weeks we decided we should move back to our respective homes although Toby had suggested we both move into my place as it was big enough. We talked about it for a while but decided we were fine on our own. He gave us both a very "policeman" speech before he agreed to let us free. Saying we must be vigilant at all times, never go out alone at night, no alleys or quiet streets without a friend etc. We agreed of course, after all he was still out there somewhere...but where!!!!

Toby had also arranged for us to have alarms fitted in our houses with a direct link to the police. We had three buttons each. The kitchen, hallway and bedroom. We giggled a little when they were fitted until Toby gave us the look that said "Don't mock, this might just save your life" !! We nodded, serious again, because of course we knew he was right but we both didn't want to keep worrying for the rest of our lives. We still kept hoping that Simon would have gone far away and into hiding but deep down we knew he would come back sometime.

I did think that maybe I should move on again but Toby had talked me out of it, he said that if Simon had found me this time he would do it again. He said we must just be really careful and with the police presence constantly there he thought we would be safe but there might be a chance of catching him if he did show. Although it could be weeks, months or even years later. I argued that we couldn't be protected for the rest of our lives but Toby had just said that hopefully they would catch him so that wouldn't be a problem.

So life went on, eyes always wide open, always being with somebody, never answering the door without checking who was out there, double locking doors and windows and phoning each other if we didn't see each other for a day or so. Lucy was convinced she would be safe as she thought it was me she was after, which was probably true but I wasn't convinced he wouldn't still try and get to her. After all, look what he did to Izzy.

Again weeks passed with no problems, sightings or any information about Simon. Life started to feel normal again. I loved working at the dog grooming salon, loved going out for lunch with Karen and spending evenings with the gang. Lilly was out of hospital and was doing really well. Tristan had been looking after her once she was home even though her mum said it wasn't necessary. She had secretly liked having Tristan around as it was only her and Lilly living in the house and having a man around, especially one that she knew her daughter was so keen on, was really nice. Lilly was still too weak to come out with the gang so we would descend on her at least once a week to let her know she wasn't forgotten.

She had taken me to one side on one such occasion and told me she didn't blame me for the attack. She had put an arm around me and said how sorry she was for everything that I had been though. This was funny coming from somebody who had just survived such a violent attack. But I understood, she must have been told the whole story about Mike etc.

Chapter THIRTEEN - (*SIMONS STORY*)

He had always been a problem child.

His mother had never married his father, in fact she wasn't sure which one of three men his father actually was. Hazel was only eighteen and living at home when she found out she was pregnant, which was no surprise to her mother and father. They had always thought she was a tart and her father had constantly told her so. Due to this awful atmosphere she drank heavily all through her pregnancy and when Simon was born her mother blamed his constant crying and attention seeking on this fact.

When Simon was six months old Hazel managed to persuade the council to allocate her a tiny flat. She was a lot happier without the hassle her parents had constantly been giving her and for a while Simon must have sensed this because he became a calmer baby, but not for long.

Hazel started a string of relationships with undesirable men and was twice caught leaving a one year old Simon in his cot alone all night. Hazel broke down and promised that it would never happen again. She must have been very convincing as they said they would let her keep the baby but were going to keep a close eye on her.

Her promise didn't last long as by the time Simon was three he was taken into care. Hazel had got involved with a crowd of junkies and was addicted to heroin, was drinking heavily again and arrested on a couple of occasions for fighting in pubs. By this time she was so far gone Simon had just become a mill stone around her neck so she was quite relieved when the social services came and took him away.

She was dead within a year having overdosed when she was too pissed to know just how much junk she was pumping into her veins.

For a few years Simon had a reasonable life. He had three foster homes and was quite used to being moved around. He had no real thoughts about having a permanent family. He just assumed that life was the way it was. When he was nine

214

the foster family he had been put with said they would like to adopt him. They had a son of their own who was a year older than Simon and they seemed to get on really well.

The family were middle clas,s with a nice detached house in the suburbs of Southampton. The father, David, owned a butchers shop and his wife, Carol, worked as a doctor's receptionist. They only had the one boy, Martin, and although they had wished for more children it had never happened. The authorities were a bit concerned that they wanted to adopt Simon just as a companion for their only son but after speaking with Simon himself away from the family he seemed quite happy with the arrangement. Even at this young age he was working it out for himself that it might be for the best. Devious as he was he thought he would get more out of the family if he 'belonged', rather than being just a temporary resident.

He was eventually adopted and changed his name officially to Burden. For a couple of years life was good. Simon got on well with Martin. Well, they had a few spats but mostly they were mates. When Martin became a teenager the family hosted a party for him. After all, thirteen is quite a big number when you get to it. They were each allowed to invite six friends and David had made up a bright colourful punch, non-alcoholic of course, and Carol had made a cake. They ordered pizzas and garlic bread and then said they would leave them all to it for a couple of hours. This was their way of saying "You are grown up now Martin and we trust you."

So David and Carol went off to the local pub feeling totally confident in leaving their boys to host a great evening. Just how wrong they could be. As soon as they were out of the door Simon opened the drinks cabinet and took out a bottle of vodka. Nobody saw him do it or saw him pour the whole bottle into the punch. He might only have been twelve but his mind was years older.

Carol opened the front door to the mayhem. It was too late to stop the mess that was awaiting them. Vomit all over the carpet, girls squealing as boys tried to grab at them, pizza boxes thrown on the floor, glasses spilled and some broken and the beautiful birthday cake she had so lovingly made tipped upside down on the settee.

Everyone was drunk with the exception of Simon. He sat quietly in the corner and said childishly "I tried to stop them but they wouldn't listen!"

Well needless to say Martin took all the blame for the evening. He tried to explain that he knew nothing about what happened, he had no idea why he and everybody else was sick and dizzy. He thought maybe there was something in the pizzas but when David tasted the punch he was not happy. Poor Martin still denied all knowledge which made it worse for him as Simon kept saying he had tried to stop him.

Two days later, after Martin was feeling better he had challenged Simon as to why he had done such a thing and worse still had blamed Martin for it. Simon had just shrugged and " You need to grow up a bit mate, learn from the master," he replied. So Martin did grow up and learn from the master.

He learned to keep as far away from Simon as possible. He learned that if anything was amiss anywhere, at school, home, in the park or football ground he would make sure he wasn't anywhere to be seen or else he would get the blame.

Simon would make sure of that. In fact Martin took to avoiding Martin like the plague. Of course David and Carol just thought it was boys of that age....they have moments when they are friends as well as when they are not.

By the time Martin was old enough and intelligent enough to go to university Simon had taken charge of the family. He had slowly overpowered them all with his wily and devious ways. Firstly they called his bluff but then just for a quiet life they tolerated him but then he took over control of the family. None of them actually realised they were being manipulated until it was too late. Martin went off to University in Bristol so he escaped but for Carol and David it was a different story.

Slowly Simon encouraged Carol to invest money into a fund that he had set up. He said it would be a great benefit for when they got older. He told her to keep it a secret from David or he might think she didn't trust that he would be able to keep them once they got to retirement age. She parted with three hundred pounds per month into an account that Simon had set up supposedly for her and David but was in fact only in his name.

He gave her papers that looked truly official and because he had them eating out of his hand by now Simon thought it was just like taking candy from a baby.

Next he targeted David. His business, he suggested when talking to David, was not going to last indefinitely, that the supermarkets would soon be the only place people would go to buy their meat. He convinced poor David that the only thing to do was to sell the shop and put the money into some sort of scheme for their future, where it would earn a good rate of interest. OK, so David was a good businessman, but Simon had such a way about him and had them so controlled that David left it all to Simon to arrange. Obviously it went into the same scheme as Carol's..Simons scheme.

By the time Simon was twenty one he had accumulated quite a huge sum of money in HIS name.

Once on one such occasion, before any of this was realised, Martin came home for Uni to find his parents both home in the afternoon. Why wasn't dad at work he had asked and once David told him that he had sold the shop Martin was a little shocked to say the least.

"But you loved having the shop" he had said.

When David explained exactly what Simon had explained to him, instead of being supportive Martin had told him he was an idiot and should have never taken advice for Simon.

"After all" he said, "what did Simon know about business, he only did two terms at tech college before he quit, how could he have learned so much from that?". It had ended in a row and with Martin heading back to Uni before the weekend was over.

A few days later, while Carol was at work David decided to check how much was in their "fund", mainly to prove to himself that he wasn't an idiot as he son seemed to think, and that there was plenty of money in their fund to look after them in years to come

.

When Carol got home from work that evening she found a very distraught David, who had obviously been crying, sitting at the kitchen table.

"Whatever is wrong" she asked him, panicking.

"Have you seen Simon?" was all he asked and when she said no she hadn't seen him for at least a week he asked "Have you ever given Simon any money, truthfully now have you"? The look on his face made her want to cry too. He looked so sad and beaten.

"Well ...er ..yes" she said "Why"?

"How much?" David almost shouted, which alarmed Carol even more.

"Oh not much, just enough for a trust fund for when we retire, why are you asking me?"

Together they sat in silence. Once Simon had moved out a month or so before it seemed that the money in the fund had moved out with him.

"What was he like when you saw him last week?" David asked. "Maybe it is just a mistake." He was clutching at straws of course but all the time there were straws to clutch he was going to reach for them.

"Well" Carol said, "maybe he was checking to see if we knew anything? He was just his normal self. Asked how we

both were, if we had planned a holiday or anything for this year"

"Ah," David jumped on this statement "he was checking to see if we had been into our fund account, maybe for holiday money or something"

Again they sat in silence.

"Are we going to be alright?" Carol asked in a quavering voice, "I mean has he taken a lot?"

"Every fucking penny" was Davids reply "Every fucking penny"

Martin was just coming out of a lecture and crossing the quadrangle when he switched on his mobile to see a new message from him mum. After the row they had been very quiet but that was a week ago so he had calmed down and hoped they had too. A message from him mum might have meant yes they had but all it said was "please come home as soon as you can" xxx Luckily Martin had a few free periods coming up and as it was only two hours or so to home he went straight this car and headed home.

222

As soon as he got to the house Carol opened the door, pulled him into the dining room well away from the lounge and in a hushed voice told him about the missing money, missing Simon and just what sort of state David was in. Martin refrained from saying anything about what he thought of Simon or their stupidity in letting him control their money but instead he just hugged him mum and said "It will be OK mum, I'll sort this out, Now where is Dad?" He found his dad sitting staring into space in the lounge. A cold cup of coffee and untouched piece of cake on the table next to him.

"I know I know" he said as soon as he heard Martin come in the room "I'm a fucking idiot, I shouldn't have trusted him, I shouldn't have been so gullible, after all I am a businessman. But son he was so persuasive, just so convincing that I was doing the right thing. Oh Martin what the fuck am I going to do?"

Martin went and sat next to his dad and put an arm around him shoulders "I'll tell you what you are going to do " he said "absolutely nothing. I am going to get this sorted, I am going to find the bastard and sort it OK ? Just trust me."

He went back into the dining room and found his mum looking anxiously at him.

"Don't worry mum" he said "like I have just told Dad I will sort this. Now where was Simon when you last saw him, I don't suppose he gave you an address by any chance?" Carol fished into her handbag an brought out a scrap of paper with an address scribbled on it.

"Here" she said. "I asked him for one when I saw him." Martin took the scrap of paper and kissing Carol on the cheek and giving her a last hug left calling back as he walked out, "I'll be in touch, and don't worry I'll get your money back for you, love you!"

These unfortunately were the last words Carol ever heard her son say. A body was found by a family out on their boat floating in the Solent about a week later. They think he died by falling from a jetty in the harbour. The post mortem showed huge quantities of alcohol in his body and a small about of cannabis. The finding was that he was drunk and a little high and had accidently fallen into the water.

Carol and David tried to protest but the science was against them. The verdict was accidental death. They suspected differently. They spoke to the police but with nothing really to go on there was not a lot they could do. The police suspected the parents were just so broken hearted that they had lost their only son......

"But wait," David had protested, "He was not our only son" then he went on to explain all about the missing money, the way Simon had disappeared. The police said kindly they would look into it but secretly Carol knew they wouldn't. She had lost he son, her money and probably a big part of husband! All due to Simon Burden. Oh how she wished she had never set eyes on him.

That was Simon's first time killing somebody and found he rather enjoyed it. When Martin had tracked him down that day and demanded that he give the money back to their parents Simon had just laughed.

"Your parents" he had smirked, "they were nothing but a bread ticket to me, you didn't think I actually cared one damn about them did you?"

225

At this point Martin had taken a swing at him and missed very badly causing him to lose balance and giving Simon a chance to grab him and throw him to the ground. Simon had not been stupid, he knew what Martin wanted when he had called at his address. Simon had been expecting one or other of the family to come around and demand their money, he was a little disappointed really that is was Martin, he was rather hoping for David so he would be able to taunt him about just how stupid he was.

He wasn't intending on killing David as deep down he felt sorry for the poor sap. He knew he would be able to send him off with a flea in his ear as he knew he wasn't mentally strong enough to stand up to him. But sadly it was Martin whom Simon despised, with his good looks and great personality and almost completed university degree. He was a hit with everyone he met. Not that Simon wasn't good looking, he really was very handsome but he had an air about him that made others slightly wary of him. With the exception of David and Carol of course. Poor weak David and Carol.

So when Martin arrived at his house Simon suggested they go for a beer to talk things over but on the way Simon had pulled Martin into an old derelict garage at the back of the pub when Martin had taken his swing and ended up on the ground with Simon on top of him. Martin was no small man but Simon was slightly bigger and a lot stronger.

He managed to drag the groggy Martin into the back room of the garage and sat him on an old swivel chair, then, grabbing some old rope he had spotted on the way in, he tied him tightly and then gagged him with his own scarf. Poor Martin was too groggy to fight back which pleased Simon as a plan was beginning to form in his devious brain. He left Martin tied up and shutting the door put a huge piece of an old car in front of it just in case anyone came by, although he doubted anyone had been near the place for ages.

Simon then went on to the pub, had a beer and bought a bottle of whiskey from the kind barmaid. She had said no to begin with as they were not supposed to sell bottles of anything but putting on some charm he had won her over. It was maybe then he might have realised that he could charm as well as manipulate anybody if he wanted to.

Walking back to the garage he fished in his pocket for the small amount of cannabis he had bought to enjoy that evening but had now decided it had a far better use. By the time he got back to the garage Martin had recovered enough to be struggling with his restraints to no avail. Simon pulled up a box and sat on it in front of Martin and rolled the joint, took off Martin's scarf and offered him a pull. Martin refused to begin with until Simon once again practiced his charm offensive and gently coerced Martin into taking a drag.

"Now" Simon said, "Let's be grown up about this", another toke "What exactly do you want me to do?" another toke.

"I want you to give our...or rather my parents their money back" Martin said.

Simon opened the bottle of whiskey and offered Martin the bottle. The Drug had started to have a mild effect on Martin as he was unused to drug taking of any description. He took the bottle and took a huge gulp.

"So," Simon continued taking a swig of whiskey himself and then handing the bottle back to Martin, "I just take the money out of my account and hand it back to David and Carol, is that what you mean?"

Martin took another toke and gulp of whiskey then went to pass the bottle and spliff back to Simon but he just waved his hand as if to say you carry on. So Martin carried on. He was almost half way down the bottle of whiskey and at the end of the joint by this time and his head was lolling.

Simon wasn't sure whether Martin was going to throw up or pass out. They had discussed the money, how Simon had promised to get it back to the Burdens. He had untied Martin in a good will gesture but he knew damn well that Martin was too far gone to do anything to him or to make a break from him. Eventually Martin keeled over and collapsed onto the floor. Perfect, thought Simon, now what to do with him?

His devious brain didn't take long to come up with a plan, about a nanosecond. He heaved Martin up and put Martin's arm around his own shoulder. Then he half dragged half carried him out of the garage. It was dark by this time and so Simon had no worries about people looking too closely at them as they walked together down towards the marina. The odd person that they passed didn't seem to notice anything untoward but just to be sure Simon said a couple of times "Come on old chap, let's get you home. Shouldn't have had that last whiskey eh !" One of the passersby just smiled knowingly as if to say "Been there, done it, know the feeling mate"

Simon went to the far end of the marina where he checked that there was nobody around, then as luck would have it he saw a boat just pulling out into the Solent so as it turned he dropped Martin into its wake. Just like that, how easy was that he thought. Martin disappeared almost at once into the surge.

"Bye bye Martin", Simon said under his breath, and "Bloody good riddance" and wondered why he felt so good. So now there was Simon, a bank full of money so he wouldn't have to work for ages, a new identity he thought might be appropriate. A move to another town too, maybe have some fun with his new found ability to lie and coerce people to do what he wanted. Oh, and an urge to kill.

Chapter FOURTEEN

Simon came into my life by accident.

I was rushing to the sandwich bar in the high street to grab a quick bite before dashing back to work to finish an important document my boss had given me. It was the day of my brother's birthday and I had spent simply ages in a card shop trying to find the best and funniest card for him. Then I had popped into the supermarket to get him a bottle of his favourite Bombay Sapphire gin. Realising I was cutting it short I had almost broken into a run, well a jog really, when I bumped straight into Simon who was gazing into the sandwich bar window.

Well I didn't know it was Simon at the time of course and now - Oh how I wish I hadn't been in such a rush that day and bumped into him! Hindsight of course it a wonderful thing.....or so they say. Anyway, I realised I had knocked the paper cup of coffee he was carrying and was mortified to see if trickle all down his jacket. I immediately apologised and offered him another cup and to maybe pay for his jacket to be cleaned. He smiled that once-winning smile of his and said of course I must pay for everything, after all it was me who did the bumping! Then with a twinkle in his eye and an even bigger smile, said "Of course not silly, I'm only joking". I warmed to him straight away so when he invited me in and offered to buy me a coffee and sandwich instead I readily accepted. That was the beginning of our, err, what would you call it, romance? Friendship or eventual devastation? You can decide.

The first few dates were fun. We just went for a drink or a burger. He told me he had been brought up in Guildford. He had loving parents. Three sisters and two brothers. His name was Simon Patterson and he was an architect for a building firm, concentrating on buying large areas of land and developing them. He designed family houses. I now realise that the only truthful piece of information in all he told me was that his name was Simon.

I, in turn, told him about my job with Mr Clever and made him laugh as I explained how he liked to pronounce it Cleever. I told him I had a brother who was married with twin boys, my father had passed away but my mother was still very much alive and well. Oh, and of course, I had a wonderful grandmother still alive and well too.

After a few dates we started to even tell each other our plans for the future. Simon wanted lots of children as he said he had had such a wonderful childhood, I agreed that it was my dream too. We almost sounded like an old married couple. I think it was then that I started to get stronger feelings for him.

He had shown no signs of jealousy or the insecurity my friend Gwen had told me about him. She had met him when we were all in the pub one night. They had obviously met before and she had told me later that she knew his ex-girlfriend and said it had been a bad breakup apparently, with him being broken hearted.

"In fact she looked a little like you Tilly" she had told me.

When I asked Simon about his ex he just dismissed it and said he had lost confidence in relationships after they broke up but he was feeling much happier about things now. He had given me a little squeeze and everything felt great. The rest of our relationship you already know about.

Now, in the wake of everything, I have found out a lot more about Simon, or the Devil as I now call him in my head. His real name is Simon, not Patterson but Burden. He never had a great childhood, he was adopted and only ever had one adoptive brother. I found all this out from Toby who had been looking through police records for information about him. Nothing had shown up in records apart from the time he had gone to the police station to say I had attacked him. He had given his name as Burden. It took a while for Toby to connect him to me. It was only that Simon had logged my name as his attacker and when Toby had drawn a blank with Simon's name he had tried mine. Bingo. Then he did a search on the name Burden and after much trolling through the internet had discovered that he was adopted and his parents lived near Southampton.

I asked if anyone had been to visit his adoptive parents and Toby said yes, the police had visited them but they knew nothing of his whereabouts, although they did have a photograph of Simon, albeit a few years ago so that was something at least. I asked if it would be OK for me to go and see them. I had no real idea why I wanted to meet them but I just felt compelled to visit. I wanted to see what type of people could bring up a child to end up a murderer, an animal who needed to be destroyed.

Toby was shocked at my vehement anger and, although agreeing with me, thought it was not really appropriate for me to visit these people, especially feeling so strongly. I on the other hand did feel it was appropriate. Their son had taken lives that should never have been taken and destroyed part of my life too, albeit I was still alive to tell the tale. After loads of persuading Toby agreed to take me over to see them but on the condition that he came in too and that if he thought I was taking things too far he would drag me out - by my feet if necessary. He said that it would have to be an off the record visit as if the investigating officers thought I was meddling there would be hell to play.

After agreeing to all his demands Toby said he would come and take me the following week.

I was nervous when we got the Burden's house. Toby had called them beforehand and asked if we could visit. They had agreed but probably had no idea why, no idea that a mad deranged woman was going to scream and shout at them for bringing up such a bastard, no idea that I intended to tell them exactly what I thought of them and that I would probably be dragged out by Toby after a few minutes.

That didn't happen.

A very frail looking man opened the door and politely welcomed us in. He wasn't the monster that I had pictured in my mind which was the first shock of the visit. The second was the sadness I could see in the eyes of both Mr and Mrs Burden. They were real, normal people, just like my mum and my dad had been. Mr Burden, who insisted we call him David, ushered us into their lounge where Mrs (or rather Carol as she insisted) sat. I looked at Toby and could see he felt the same as me.

"Was there something more you needed to know?" David was asking Toby but he just pointed to me and explained just who I was. The look on their faces said it all. Carol started to cry and nervously shrunk away when I approached her to put an arm around her. It was so very obvious that these poor people were suffering. After all they had to live with the fact that their son, even though an adoptive son so did not carry any of their genes, was a killer. David stood up and said he would make some tea. Carol continued to cry softly but eventually let me put an arm around her, then suddenly she grabbed me and broke into huge uncontrollable sobs, holding onto me really tightly. My heart was breaking seeing this poor woman breaking down and I realised I had totally misjudged these people.

Once the tea arrived and Carol's sobs had subsided a little we sat quietly sipping at it. Not saying anything for what seemed like ages, then suddenly David said "He killed our son too you know". At this we all looked up.

Toby put his mug down and looking directly at David asked "Why would you think that David ?"

"It's true" he said. "Oh, the police at the time said it was an accident but we know it wasn't."

"Hang on a minute" Toby butted in "Was this your son who drowned, the thought was that he must have fallen in the Solent? Didn't they find evidence of drugs and alcohol in his blood" Wow I thought, Toby has really been doing his homework, I had no idea about this.

"Yes" David continued and Carol started to softly cry again "We explained to the police at the time that Martin never drank whiskey and was totally against drugs. The only way he would have even considered either of these was if he was in a situation where it warranted him to do it. OR and I say OR he was persuaded by somebody who had a way of persuading people to do things they really didn't want to" he looked over at Carol now.

"He took all our money you know" she said "everything we had worked for, persuaded us to put it in a so called saver's fund for later years, then he took the lot and disappeared. Martin went to find him and a week later we are told Martin is dead" tears streamed down her face and she let me cuddle her again.

"Why didn't the police investigate it then?" Toby was asking "I mean surely they had enough information to link Martin drowning to Simon taking your money?"

"We tried to tell them but I don't know if they really believed just how much we lost. They were quite happy to believe he was a university student who had been on the drink and fell into the water"

"Well they sure as hell are going to investigate it now!" Toby was really angry I could see.

David looked at Carol and half smiled, "Maybe at last darling," he said, "somebody will believe us"

One the way home we chatted constantly about everything and nothing. Firstly of course we went thought everything we had learned from Carol and David, then compared just what we thought of them. We both agreed they were very nice people, very sad and had no idea just what Simon was capable of other than stealing their money. We were convinced they had no knowledge of his whereabouts and Toby said he was definitely going to see what could be done about re opening the case of Martin's death, although deep

239

down he said he knew that unless they find Simon and he confesses to killing Martin there was very little likelihood of changing the coroner's report of accidental death, but he would try for the sake of Carol and David.

About halfway home Toby suggested we stop for a bite to eat, "there is a nice little pub not far from here" he said and just as he said it we saw a sign for the Fur and Feathers two miles right.

Once seated and settled with a drink in front of me I started, for the first time ever, to study Toby. He was at the bar ordering our food and as he turned to come back to our table a very tiny flutter shot though my tummy.

We had a lovely meal and I was on my third glass of wine before Toby suddenly looked at his watch and said we should be making a move. I was quite happy sitting there but poor Toby had only had a glass of lemonade and a coffee and was probably right. After all he had to get me home and then drive all the way back to Guildford.

I don't know if it was the wine or the earlier flutter in my tummy but I couldn't take my eyes off him as we drove along. After a few minutes he suddenly said "You felt it too eh" he put a hand on my knee and gave it a squeeze then took it away immediately. In return I did the same to him. We were silent for a while then I said "Would it be wrong? I mean because of Mike, would it spoil things, would the guilt be too great?"

"Do you think so" he said "do you not think that if Mike was still here, you would be married and happy, but he is not. Do you really think he would want you to be sad for the rest of your life? And do you not think that he would be happier knowing you are with a good man? I mean me by the way!"

I put my hand back on his knee and left it there for the rest of the journey.

Chapter FIFTEEN

Toby didn't go back to Guildford that night, in fact he didn't go back the next night either. We didn't go to bed together on that first night, we just sat and talked and talked. I suppose having known Toby for so long and having gone through so much together is just didn't feel right, but by the next day we had got over our inhibitions and fell into each other's arms.

It had now been three whole years since Mike and the "event." Toby and I went from strength to strength, so much so that I decided to move back to Guildford and in with Toby. It meant Karen having to find a new receptionist for the grooming parlour but she said she would rather I was happy than worry about my job.

"Anyway," she said, "you were rubbish, I can get a better receptionist anyday!"

I knew she was joking and joined in with "I hated the bloody job anyway!"

Well we had a little leaving party. The gang all came to the pub - even Lilly, who was so much better.

"I will miss you all terribly" I said "I hope you will all come and visit" Of course they all said they would but we all knew they wouldn't. Well I rather hoped Lucy would as we had been so close for so long. She had a new man in her life. Phillip was a lovely man and I believed him when he promised to bring her up for a visit.

There was no word about Simon, hadn't been for so long now that we had all got to the stage where we thought he would never be found. I had convinced myself that he had moved on and was no longer searching for me and wanting to kill me. I did think though in low moments that there was probably somebody else out there who might be going through the same thing as me. I really hoped that he hadn't killed again although I feared it, he was so obviously mad.

Toby and I had been living together for about three months when life changed again.

Being a detective Toby had a lot of friends and colleagues littered around the country. People he had been on courses with and who had become friends, people who maybe worked with him and moved on and people who worked on cases with him where there had been nationwide searches., one of which was the search for Simon of course.

We had a call one evening from a girl called Sally who had worked on a kidnap case with Toby a few years ago and they had kept in touch and although she lived and worked in Bristol she was also involved in the nationwide search for Simon. After the pleasantries about how we all were, and how her family was, she came to the point.

Apparently, she had told Toby, a woman had come into the Bridewell Police station in the centre of Bristol saying she had been attacked by her boyfriend. Well normally Sally said she wouldn't have been involved in a domestic but while she was talking to a colleague near where the woman was making her statement she overheard the police officer dealing with her saying that her boyfriend had already been in making a statement saying she had attacked him.

244

"Well" she said "that rang a bell, so I fished out the identikit picture and a copy of the photograph of Simon and showed it to the woman. Toby it was him. She said he had now shaved his head and had a little goatee beard but it was definitely Simon.

Toby thanked her and arranged to go down to Bristol to interview the woman. He asked Sally to ensure the woman was taken to a safe house just in case. Sally said she would sort it and arrange for the woman, named Yasmin, to come in for an interview the next day.

"I want to come too, would that be OK" I asked Toby. "Can't see any reason why not, but you will have to stay in the background unless I need you for comparisons in his actions, is that OK?"

We were both quiet after the call. I didn't know what to think, whether I was pleased there might be a chance of catching him or worried in case he got away again. Toby tried to concentrate of the TV show we were watching before she called but I could see he wasn't really watching. I went to the kitchen and came back in with a bottle of wine and two glasses.

"If we have a busy day tomorrow let's have a relaxing evening tonight".

Toby smiled, and opening the wine bottle, winked and said "You always know what to do don't you. I love you Tilly."

I snuggled up beside him on the settee and said "I love you too Toby. Now let's drink our wine and watch the show, tomorrow is another day, and at least we will be facing it together."

The next morning we headed down to Bristol. I had never been there before and what a pleasant surprise I got when we got there. We were a little too early to go to the police station so we walked down Corn street and stopped in one of the old buildings, which I think must have once been a bank, and had a coffee and bun. We were both a little nervous, well I was, just the thought of speaking to somebody else who had been involved with the Devil and come out alive sent shivers down my spine again.

I sat outside the interview room while Toby and Sally went in to speak with Yasmin. They didn't need to call me in so I sat there for the duration of the interview doing Sudoku puzzles, or rather trying as I found it really difficult to concentrate knowing they were just a wall or two away. Eventually the door opened and Sally came out followed by, what could only be described as my doppelganger. Toby came up behind them and looked straight at me. I could see he was watching for my reaction and I certainly gave him one. Sally nodded to me and Yasmin looked, no stared at me. She obviously saw the resemblance. Honestly it was like looking into a mirror. She stopped and asked if Sally minded if she had a few words with me.

"You survived too then" she said in a quavering voice. "You know, he used to call me Matilda and I had no idea why until today. My god I had no idea what he was, he seemed so nice when I first met him."

I just nodded. What could I say. We both knew exactly what he was now. "Good luck" I said and held my hand out to shake hers but she just put her arms around me and hugged me like we were sisters or something.

"At least I found out in time thanks to you" she said.

"Yes, but if you didn't look like me he might have left you alone" was all I could think of to say. She turned then and followed Sally. "Sally," I called out and as she turned "Look after her please." Sally nodded and smiled and they disappeared.

On the ride back Toby filled me in on the interview. Apparently they had met in a pub. He had accidently spilled his drink on her as she stood at the bar.

"OMG that rings a bell!" I said and reminded Toby of how I had met him. I did the spilling that time so he probably got the idea from then. Anyway, Toby said they went out a few times. He told her loads of rubbish about him being a teacher this time. He said he came from a big happy family but had been hurt by his last girlfriend so was very cautious with any new relationships. She said he seemed so genuine.

"You know Toby" I said "I am thinking that maybe some of his madness comes from him having a bad childhood and wishing he did have a big family and everyone was happy. I don't mean with Carol and David, they both did their best, but before they adopted him. Didn't you say he had been pushed from pillar to post prior to them? It certainly doesn't condone anything that he has done but it might have something to do with his madnesss."

"Well" he said "It is in the hands of the Bristol force now to try and find him, only I don't expect they will have any more luck than we did. I really wish they would though, I would feel a lot happier when I know you are totally safe from him. My God, did you see the resemblance between you and Yasmin? You could almost have been twins!"

"I know what" I said, "Let's forget all about it for a couple of hours and how about I take you to dinner, somewhere between here and Guildford, where we will be on strange turf and no ghosts lurking. A deal ?"

"Do you know Tilly, I love you more every minute" was all he said and pulled off the motorway in search of a village where we might find a nice gastro pub or similar.

We did have a nice evening which was a surprise after the events of the day. I think as Toby knew Sally was on the case and Yasmin was in a safe house he was a bit more relaxed. I, on the other hand was not quite so. Did it mean that Simon was still after me? It surely couldn't be a coincidence that he just managed to drop his drink over somebody who looked just like me, could it? I knew the answer to that alright. So that means he is still obsessed and is still out to kill me, fucking hell - will I ever be free?

The answer to that question came sooner than I thought.

A week after our trip to Bristol Toby had the weekend off so we decided to go to the country. We found a supposedly medieval hotel online just outside Bath which looked amazing so I booked two nights. Unfortunately when we arrived the hotel was not quite what we were expecting. We parked in what we thought was a farmers' field but it did say hotel parking. We had to climb over a wheelbarrow and round a cement mixer to get to the door. The musty smell once inside was enough to put us off so we turned around and headed off to Bath city centre. Not where we were intending to stay but once there we found a nice hotel that luckily had a room so we booked in there. We held hands as we strolled around Bath, taking in the knick knacks in the quaint shop windows, and agreeing that maybe it was a good thing that the other hotel was rubbish.

Then suddenly we rounded a corner and there he was....standing on the bank looking over the weir, it was Simon. I knew instantly as he is a tall man and slim, but with rather large ears that you can't help but notice, as soon as I saw the now beginning to grow head of hair and the goatee I had no doubt. He hadn't seen me so I grabbed Toby and pulled him sideways behind an ice cream vendor

"You want an ice cream?" he asked thinking I was messing with him, "We've only just had lunch!"

Then he saw the look on my face and realised something had happened.

"He's over there" I said pointing towards the bank "Leaning over looking at the weir."

"Who?" Toby asked then realising who it had to be started to pull out his phone."You sure it's him?"

"Positive" I said.

Quickly he called Sally, I know Bristol is only about thirteen miles from Bath and if we could keep an eye on him without his seeing us it would give them time to get here, or at least alert the Bath police. Toby put his phone back in his pocket and whispered that they were on their way and had also alerted the Bath police. We sneaked a look around the corner to check if he was still there, he was which was good thing as we could hopefully follow him.

He lead us through a maze of people, down the side of the famous Baths and towards the park behind. Toby had his phone in his hand now and was giving instructions to Sally and her team. Then Simon just disappeared. He was there one second and gone the next.

"Shit, shit, shit!" Toby was whispering down the phone, "He's just vanished!" but just as he was saying it he fell to the ground.

I spun around to come face to face with the Devil. I screamed as loud as I could hoping the phone would pick up my voice.

"He's here! Man down! Man down!" was all I could think of to say. Stupid as maybe but I had seen so many cop shows in my life I thought they would understand the lingo. Simon tried to grab me but I fought him off with my bag then I remembered I had a rape alarm in it and some perfume. While he was trying to grab at me, my bag fell open and the rape alarm miraculously fell to the ground.

Toby was lying there next to it, stunned but alive. He grabbed at the alarm and set it off.

Within seconds people started to appear. Simon started to run letting go of me, then as if by magic there was a huge man heading toward us and he took him down like I have never seen anybody do before. He just picked Simon off the ground and threw him down so hard he was obviously winded, then sat on top of him, just like that.

Everyone who had gathered around applauded. One lady come rushing up to us asking if I was OK thinking it was just mild mugging with the thief trying to grab my handbag. I just nodded and pointed to poor dazed Toby who had sat up by this time and was holding the back of his head. The police sirens were getting closer.

"Was he trying to rob you, my luvver?" the man sitting on top of Simon said.

"No, not rob" I said. "You won't believe what you have done, he is wanted for several murders!"

The man looked stunned but didn't move so Simon was helpless. Then within seconds I saw uniforms arriving and Sally, lovely Sally. Several uniformed officers were dragging Simon away. Another was taking a statement from the man who had been sitting on him, and I, I was crying and cradling Toby in my arms.

The lady said she was a nurse and looked at his head and said that he was lucky that apart from a small gash it appeared to be just a big bump, but he should go and get checked in case he had concussion. I promised to take him to the hospital straight away and so she went off happy.

"He must have spotted us" I said "It looks like he was carrying some kind of truncheon or similar with him. I'm sure they'll find whatever he hit you with on him when they get him back to the station. Now I must get you checked over. Please come with me sir" I said in a mock police voice which made him smile at last. "We've got him, I said "At last we've got him, I can't believe is was so easy in the end" Sally come over then and once she could see Toby was OK she said she would call us in the morning and let us know what was happening.

"Go get checked and get a good night's sleep" she said and then as she walked off, turned back to say "Well done, wrong way to go about it but heh.. great result"

"Love you too" Toby called as she disappeared.

After much protest I took Toby to A&E. where they checked him over and just said as long as he doesn't get any headaches or dizziness in the next twenty four hours he should be fine, but if he does he should come back.

"See I told you " he said " I'm fine! But hey, do you realise that he is in custody? Actual custody, Tilly? That means that unless he escapes, we or rather you are free!"

Until I heard those words it hadn't really dawned on me. I mean it was a bit of a comedy really, the way the big man had stopped Simon and the way he had not only stopped him but held him by sitting on him. If he wasn't such a dangerous murderer if would have been comical. Still the end of the story was that he had stopped Simon by whatever way he did and it worked, and now the Devil was in the cells and hopefully staying in a cell for the rest of his life.

It suddenly hit me like I had been pole-axed....I was free, I was free. NO more worrying about where he was going to show up next and who was going to be his next victim. The hugeness of it all was amazing.

I looked over at Toby as I was parking outside the hotel, his head was lolling back a little and I was frightened until he suddenly sat up and said "Let's celebrate...after all we came here for some fun and a break, let's go for it. He can't be around any corner now, he can't hurt you anymore darling. It's a new life for you, me, us and I don't want to wait another moment to start living it."

We went back to our room in the hotel, showered, which took quite some time as we did it together, then dressed and went out for a meal to celebrate. Oh, what a relief it was to really know he wasn't going to be around anymore, not for a very long time if ever!

Chapter SIXTEEN

After a wonderful and slightly drunken meal in the hotel restaurant we wandered back to our room, giggling and swaying slightly as we went. So very happy but also so very sad. Once back in the room Toby put his arms around me and pulled me close.

"Tilly" he said "I know this was never our intention, I mean to end up together like this"

"Oh my god," I thought to myself, "He's going to call it a day with me. I thought he loved me!".

As the shiver went down my spine awful thoughts spun through my head. I started thinking I was going to be alone again. How could he do this to me, tears were beginning to sting in my eyes, I pulled away from him so he wouldn't see but then I suddenly realised that Toby was still speaking, asking me something.

"What?" I thought. "Whhhaaaatt" I said, as I hadn't heard anything he had said other than the initial "Tilly, I know it was never our intention."

"I'm asking you to be my wife, weren't you listening? Come on Tilly, please say you'll marry me!"

I didn't need to reply, I just kissed him really hard and then again and again. He pulled me over to the bed and we made wonderful love all through that night, well a lot of it anyway. I know deep down I should maybe have been feeling that I was being unfaithful to Mike's memory but it all felt so right. I didn't feel guilty at all. After all Mike was gone, I could never do anything about that, the bastard who killed him was in jail. Toby and I had never any intentions of being together until the past couple of months and as Toby said, he would hope that Mike would be happy for us.

It all seemed like a dream, although at times feelings of déjà vu occurred. Especially when I started organising the wedding.

Although we had decided to make it totally low key there were still loads of things to think about. It would be in

Guildford registry office, and after we would all go for a meal in a local restaurant. We also made stag and hen nights a definite no-no.

We decided we would only invite my mum, brother Tom, Casandra and their children. I wanted my lovely gran to come but she had had a fall and was nursing a bad hip. The nursing home said she was better left there so I said I would go and see her directly after the wedding to show her my dress and take her some cake. The other guests were going to be Lucy, her new man and Karen of course. Sally from the station in Bristol and a couple of people from the station where Toby worked.

Sadly, as Toby's parents lived in New Zealand, they said it would be impossible to come. His father was a professor at Christchurch University and he was in the middle of a crucial exam period so they couldn't get away, but sent us a huge cheque to buy ourselves something special they had said, rather than them send us something we may not really like. I had met with them through Skype on a couple of occasions and had promised we would go and visit as soon as we could.

The night before the big day was weird. Things suddenly started to zoom around in my brain. I wouldn't let Toby out of my sight that night. I held him close and pushed the horrible thoughts, that were trying to ruin my day to come, out of my mind.

We both woke early, although I don't think either of us slept a wink really. Lying still and trying to hear if the other was breathing heavily as in sleep or lightly as if awake but just thinking. Neither of us liked to ask the other in case we actually were asleep.

We laughed when we realised the next morning that we had both been awake all the time. Toby went off to get some coffee and Danish from Starbucks while I lay in a hot scented bubble bath enjoying every moment. I must have been dozing because all of a sudden I woke in a panic, somebody was breathing over me...screaming I sat up and opened my eyes. Petrified of what I was going to see. After my attack by Simon in the bath I very rarely took baths, just stuck to showers.

"Sweetheart, whatever is wrong" Toby's gentle voice drifted though my screams "I brought your coffee up for you but you looked so peaceful I hardly wanted to wake you, thought I would wait until the water got too cool then wake you, or I might just have got in with you!"

"Oh I'm so sorry darling" I sobbed "I must have been dreaming, it was like the day the Devil came in and I was in the bath" He grabbed the big towel from the radiator and lifting me gently from the bath wrapped it around me.

"I will look after you forever, you know that don't you, you must never be frightened again, not all the time I have breath in my body."

"Please god" I said "don't ever let Simon get out of prison" "He'll never get out" Toby said "I promise, and that is one promise I will never break, now get your glad rags on we have a wedding to go to – remember?"

"I love you so much" was all I could think of to say.

Our wedding day was the best day ever. We had decided it wasn't to be tinged with any kind of sadness. It was to be our day, a new beginning at last for us both. The sun had come out to say a big Hi-Five to us and wish us well. The registrar was a wonderful woman who made us all giggle, she had a slight lisp which made her remarks even funnier. The twins were little dreamboats dressed in identical little suits with one in a red bow tie and one in a blue one.

"Is that so we can tell them apart" Toby had whispered to me when they walked in?"

"Russell is the one with the red tie" I whispered back.

"Got it" he said.

I had bought a new dress of course, I couldn't even think to wear the one I had bought for my wedding to Mike. That had been wrapped in tissue paper and put in a memory box, never to be worn or probably even taken out of the box for ever. I had chosen a bright pink dress and I loved all the admiring looks I got from passers-by as I walked down the street to the registery office withToby at my side. He looked amazing and so happy I wanted to cry. Everyone in fact looked wonderful. Sally had brought her husband Pete and their eldest girl Laura who was fifteen and took an immediate liking to the twins, which gave Tom and Cassandra a break during the meal, as she insisted on taking the boys outside to the swings after they had finished eating. Tom made a short but lovely speech and then it was

Toby's turn to thank everybody for coming etc. There were no horrible moments of sadness or remembering. We all seemed to put the past behind us, for that day anyway.

After the speeches Toby gave me an envelope.

"Go on" he said. "Open it." It was a ticket for me to travel first class to New Zealand.

My eyes nearly popped out of my head when I saw it, ""But this must have cost a fortune" I said "and it's only for one person."

"I know I know " he said "but the date for the trial has been set"

I had not known that. Simon was still on remand as they had so much information to collate I thought the trial would be ages yet. I had to give more statements just to ensure nothing was missed out . They didn't want any chance of him getting off with any of the terrible crimes he had committed.

They must have told Toby the trial date before he bought the ticket and I think he wanted me out of the way, it was in six weeks time, the same time as the date on the ticket..

"I can't get away until after the trial and my folks so want to meet you. I will follow as soon as I can get away I promise."

But that would mean I would only have six weeks with my darling new husband before we would be apart for god knows how long. He saw the look of doubt on my face, part of me was really excited at the prospect of going to New Zealand but part of me was saying no, stay with Toby.

"I understand what you are thinking" he said "but I promise if the trial gets adjourned or delayed indefinitely I will get the earliest flight over I possibly can. Go enjoy yourself, my parents will give you a great time, I am sure of that!"

"I'm sorry to look as though I don't appreciate it, I do" I said "it's just that I will miss you."

"And I'll miss you too of course but hey, we have the rest of our lives to be with each other eh? Now come on and give your new husband a kiss."

"OK" I said "I'll go to New Zealand but I want you to promise to come out as soon as you possibly can."

"Of course I will, silly," he said" do you think I want to be away from my wife a minute longer than necessary? Never!"

After the meal Toby took me to my grandmother in the nursing home. She had never met Toby before but obviously approved because as soon as we walked in her aged brown watery eyes suddenly started to twinkle.

"So" she said "this is the young man who has stolen my darling granddaughter's heart, come here and let me have a good look at you!"

The visit went very well, she loved my dress and ate the cake with the tea the nurse brought us. I told her the story, briefly, of her clock and how I always felt she was looking out for me. She seemed sad but just said that of course she always was, but was sad because she couldn't be there in person. At this point Toby took her hand and held it while he said that even though she may not be, that he would be, and she had no need to worry. Between her thoughts and his presence I would be looked after forever.

On our way out Gran called me back while Toby carried on walking.

"He is wonderful" she said "I love him, he will make you happy I know it. Please come and see me again soon" I gave her a big hug and kiss.

Once outside Toby said "Seal of approval? Please say yes"

"Oh yes" I said "she loved you!"

We agreed to do lots of things in the six weeks we had together. Every time Toby had some free time at work he would call me and when he had hours or half days off we would go to lunch, the park even bowling although he was too good, I decided we should go ice skating instead as he was hopeless at that.

We planned what we would do after our visit to New Zealand. We would get a puppy, or a dog from the rescue home I said as I would rather do that. He agreed, maybe a cat too as he loved cats. Then maybe in a year or so when we were settled we could maybe think about starting a family. I wanted four children but when Toby screwed his face up at that I said "Only two then?"

"Nah", he had said, "I want a football team, at least ten!"

We were so comfortable with each other as we made our plans. He didn't want me to go to work, for a while at least, he said. It wasn't worth getting a job anyway until after our trip which was fine by me. I loved playing the little housewife.

A week or so after the wedding we were curled p on the sofa watching a movie when the door bell went.

"Sally, what a lovely surprise" I said as I opened it. "Come on in." We all sat in down the lounge.

"Ok" Sally started with, after the polite chit chat about the wedding and how lovely it was etc, "It isn't really a social call I'm afraid."

"Come on Sally spit it out" Toby said "I know you, it must be something no good, to come all this was without calling first"

"Well" she said "You know there has been a lot of publicity since Simon's arrest. Well there have been the usual phone calls telling all sorts of tales about him. You know how people love to get involved. Some of them knew him from school, some lived near or whatever. Well some - four to be precise, have actually got a real story to tell. They were all assaulted by Simon. Two of them really badly. We are currently investigating their claims but it does seem like they are genuine. I wondered if you guys would come down to Bristol and be with us at an interview with these women. I know it is a lot to ask Tilly and I don't want you getting upset but I think that if there are a lot of similarities between theirs and your story, then we will have more chance of getting their assaults taken into account. We do believe them but obviously there is no proof, as their assaults happened more than two years ago. But if they say some of what happened is exactly as it happened to you then maybe their stories can be used in evidence."

I looked at Toby who looked as shocked as me, but he nodded a reassuring nod so I agreed to go to Bristol.

Chapter SEVENTEEN

It felt really strange meeting women who had gone through similar experiences to me. Obviously they didn't have the memory of a dead fiancé, a dead best friend or a stranger who may or may not have looked like me, and a new friend who had a similar name. But they had the same contact that I had and the same aggression.

We all sat together in an interview room. Sally had brought us coffees and biscuits. If it hadn't been such a serious issue it would almost have been laughable. A bit like an old school reunion of jilted girlfriends.

It wasn't until we had all sat together for a few minutes that it started to dawn on us, all more or less at the same time. We all looked alike. I mean we all had different length hair, and in slightly different styles but we were all about the same build, same height and weight. In fact if you dressed us all identically and lined us up you wouldn't be surprised if people thought we were sisters.

"This is crazy" Sally suddenly said "I hadn't even noticed you girls were so alike until I had you in the same room together. She immediately pulled up the pictures she had on her phone of Izzy, Lucy and Lilly and also the poor girl who was murdered near to my work. The likeness was uncanny.

"So maybe the reason he went after Lilly wasn't because he thought it might be me with a name change" I stammered. "It was because she looked like the rest of us, Bloody hell girls you had a real escape"

We all compared statements. Yes he was lovely and kind to begin with, although a little jealous, but once he felt feelings for him growing he turned nasty.

Phillipa was beaten because she didn't cook his eggs properly; Tracy, because she was late home; Suzie because she dared mention a colleague at work had said she looked pretty that day. None of them had reported it at the time as he had told then he was leaving them and would get treatment and come back once he was better.

Yeah like fuck !!!!!

Now the thoughts turned to why, why was he after us at all?

"I may have a hunch" Toby said "But I will need to do some research, and if I'm right I can answer your question and have a good reason for his madness."

"Wel,l are you going to fill us in?" We all echoed.

"As soon as I have it confirmed in my mind. Guys you have been great coming here today to give your statements. Luckily we don't need to hide you away in any safe house as Simon is in custody but if you wouldn't mind I'll leave it there until I have had done a little more research."

We all agreed to meet as soon as Toby had found out a few things. We all hugged as if we had known each other for years and said we would see each other soon.

 "What's this bloody hunch then mate?" Sally said after they had gone.

"I think we need to go and see David and Carol, again" was all he said. "Come on then, there is no time like the present!"

We went in Toby's car with Sally following in hers as it was quite a way from Bristol to Guildford. Just as we were approaching the Surrey borders Toby got me to call the Burdens and say we had a few questions for them if they didn't mind answering. They of course said that would be no problem and that they would get the kettle on.

We pulled up outside their house about forty minutes later. Toby insisted we stop in a Tesco Express on the way and buy a cream cake. After all, he had said, they are lovely people and I'll bet they will have a plate full of biscuits at the ready for when we get there.

He was right of course, as soon as we were in their front door we were ushered into the lounge where there was a tray with a pot of tea, cups and a plate with chocolate cookies on it, oh and the obligatory doily. I immediately thought of my mum, that is exactly what she would do in this situation.

I gave Carol the cake we had brought and she was delighted. She rushed off to the kitchen and returned with it on a plate, with another doily of course, some small plates, pastry forks and a cake knife.

After the introductions to Sally we all sat and waited while Carol served us with tea and slices of the cake, then after a few mouthfuls and comments of "hmm, delicious", Toby got to the point.

"Do you by any chance have any pictures of Simon's birth mother?" he asked. He then went on to explain the similarities in Simons victims. He explained his theory about how he thought that maybe Simon's mother had been similar too and that is what had set off this madness in him.

"But he hadn't seen her since before he was eight" Carol said "would he remember her that well?"

"Children can remember lots of things" Sally said "especially really good or really bad memories. Some children will blot it out completely but others will dwell on it and then suddenly it erupts. I have seen it loads of times. Something triggers them off, like maybe, as Toby thinks, the sight of someone similar to their abuser or somebody who had taunted them, or just a sudden recognition of something that happened in their past."

The Burdens looked at each other, "I don't think I've ever seen a picture, have you Carol?" David said.

Carol thought for moment.

"Well" she began, "I remember when he first arrived here he had a little toy suitcase, you know the kiddie ones made of plastic with a little lock and key. I'm sure he had one of those, red it was, yes that's right, red with stickers on it. Well I remember thinking poor little lost boy, that is all he has of his past. He never let me look inside it though. I asked him what was in it but he had clutched it close to him and said it was his, I never saw it again. To be honest I felt so sorry for the little lad that I didn't mention it after that and until now I had completely forgotten about it. Do you think he may have had something like a picture of his mum in that?"

"Well possibly" Toby said "Have you any idea where that case is now ?"

Again Carol thought.

"Well wouldn't he have taken it with him when he left home if it was all he had of his early life?" she said. "Unless"....she jumped up and disappeared. They heard a few squeaks and crashes a small scream and then a voice cursing "Bloody thing!" David jumped up but before he could leave the room Carol returned clutching a tiny kiddie toy suitcase covered in dust.

"Voila!" she said "It was in the loft" and handed it to Toby.

W all watched on as Toby broke the fastened lock. There was no key attached like there is usually - you know, the little chain that holds two keys when you buy these things. Inside was an assortment of tiny objects and some pieces of paper but no photograph. Toby emptied the contents out onto the coffee table. It was a surreal moment. There, in front of them all, was the entire past of an eight year old child, which was really sad - but also the entire past of an eight year old child turned murderer. There were three green plastic soldiers, each holding a gun. Four plastic farm animals, a couple of pieces of Lego and a hair band but the saddest thing of all was a crude child's stick drawing of a person, well a woman supposedly as it had a type of triangle shaped dress on, and....

"Oh my God – what's he drawn in her hand? Is that a needle?" Carol said looking at the drawing.

We all sat in silence for a moment or two until Sally said "And we wonder why people go insane"

On the way home Toby squeezed my knee with a sort of reassuring squeeze and said he was still sure he was right about the mother, we will just have to dig a bit more, there must be a picture of his mother somewhere.

Time was slipping by quite quickly and suddenly it was only three weeks until I was going to New Zealand, or more importantly maybe, until the trial.

Sally had tried to locate a picture of Simon's mother, as had we, but with no luck. We had gone through all her family members one by one but none of them had any pictures. It was a very sad little life she had led, the poor woman. Giving birth so young with no support from friends or family and then getting involved with the wrong crowd who got her into drugs and eventually led to her demise at such a young age. Poor woman, nothing to show for her short life other than her murderous offspring.

Surely, I had said to Toby, if she was involved in drugs and had ever been arrested there would be something on file but he had said she may have been pulled in but never charged. How about the newspapers, I had suggested hopefully, she could have been involved in something that had made the news? Still we drew a blank. By this time we had decided that there was no chance of this link ever being confirmed. That maybe we would never find out just why he did such terrible things.

Toby had it in his head that if he could prove it was due to the resemblances' to his mother, Simon had taken so much care to single out the women he did abuse, attack and even murder. They were only chosen for that reason and nothing to do with them being who they were. Me included, maybe at least my guilt would ease too.

"So if they decide he is not mad due to his childhood experiences he will probably go jail where there is always a chance some do gooder in years to come will get him released before he is a hundred?" I asked Toby, "But if they suspect he is mad, or if we can show a link, he would probably be put into Broadmoor for the rest of his life. I know which I would prefer."

"No nothing like that my darling" he said "I just feel I owe it to Phillipa, Suzie etc and you of course, to give you an explanation

We had given up completely until one week before I was due to leave for New Zealand. I had a call from David one afternoon while Toby was at work, asking if there was any chance we could go down to see them, he sounded a bit excited on the phone - although I wasn't sure if it was good excitement or something else. Anyway I duly agreed that we would go down that evening.

"I bet they want to wish you a happy holiday or something" Toby said as we drove to their house, "Probably baked you a bon voyage cake or something!" we both laughed at the thought of a cake in the shape of an aeroplane with my name on the side. We sort of had been adopted by Carol and David as we had got to know them. Now they had no son of their own to lavish their affection on, Toby had become a replacement and I had become an added bonus.

We arrived and were welcomed as usual by David ushering us into the lounge. We sort of almost expected the entire neighbourhood to be waiting inside and shouting "Surprise!" and "Happy Holidays!" This couldn't have been further from the truth.

David started. "When Simon disappeared we left his room as was just in case he came back, but once we realised what he had done with our money we threw out all his stuff. We didn't want him to ever come back. Well then you guys showed up and told us of all the terrible things he had done."

"And so we decided to -" Carol chipped in but David shushed her, giving her a "please let me tell them" look, he obviously wanted to tell the story himself. Carol just smiled and motioned her head as if to say go on then.

"So, as I say" he continued" once you guys filled us in," Even I was getting a bit impatient by now and was dying to hear what they had to tell us, I almost butted in myself but held back. "So yes, now where was I, oh yes as I say we didn't want any part of that monster left in our house so we decided to completely redecorate his old bedroom. Well that

279

was weeks ago now but it was only yesterday that the new carpet eventually arrived. The fitters were upstairs pulling the old one up when one of them said I had a loose floorboard. So out I go to the shed to get my hammer and nails" I could feel Toby getting a bit restless by this point but he said nothing. "I went upstairs and found the board that was loose and pulled it up so I could re-sit it and that's when I saw it."

"Saw what?" we both almost screamed at the same time.

"THIS......" Carol was there with an excited look on her face. She held out her hand to display a piece of what looked like screwed up paper. She handed it to Toby who at once realised straight away that it was a photograph. Very screwed up but that had been very carefully smoothed out by, I suspect, Carol. There she was, Simon's mother. There was no doubt that it was her as she looked exactly like me.

On the back in very spidery and childlike writing were the words "*I WILL KILL YOU.*"

David looked so pleased with himself, as if he had done something to be very proud of. Well he had, hadn't he. He had found something, although by a total fluke, but something that we would never have found and the answer to the question as to why.

"He must have had such a sad time with his mother, I'm not saying I blame her for everything. She must have had a rough time being on her own so young and with a baby to look after"

"Well, Tilly, you might be right," David said. "But she might have been a baddie too."

"I suppose we shall never know" Carol said " but what we do know is that we lost our beloved son due to this monster."

"And all our savings" David chipped in, looking down instantly when he got a withering look from his wife.

Money. Important yes, but nothing compared to loosing the one you love. Toby immediately looked at me and saw the tears streaming down my face.

Carol noticed too and suddenly realising that we were both sharing the same horrendous sorrow she decided she must change the subject swiftly before we all started crying.

She stood up and before we could say anything she said "David and I would like you both to come to dinner with us tonight. I have a reservation in a restaurant in the centre of town. It will be our belated wedding present to you and our treat."

Toby and I looked at each other, what could we say but "That would be wonderful"

I cleaned my face in Carol's bedroom. She sat me at her dressing table mirror and gave me some wet wipes and tissues. She pulled up a second chair next to me and did the same to herself as her tears had begun too. We both sat at that mirror, remembering our past loves. Mine a fiancé and hers a son. We had a bond, we both knew that.

"Come on" she said after a moment or two "memories are wonderful things but must not get in the way of the future. They are to be cherished and brought out on certain occasions, but not to bring sadness." I totally agreed with that, so off we went downstairs to join the boys.

The evening turned out to be really rather fun. We had a delicious meal which we tried to pay for but were totally not allowed. We talked about things to do in New Zealand, about Toby's parents, about my mum, my brother and his darling twins. About how they had been so looking forward to Martin leaving University to see just what he would do with his life, or rather what he would have done. I glanced at Carol when this conversation started but she simply smiled gently and nodded. Memories on certain occasions she whispered, can be good. We didn't mention Simon, after all, why would we need the Devil at their dinner table. We left promising to keep in touch and visiting once we had come back from New Zealand.

"I think that went well" I said in the car on the way home.
"I saw your tears" Toby said. "I am so sorry, but I will make your life whole again I promise."
"Toby" I said "I loved Mike with all my heart, and I will miss him forever but I'm in love with you now, you are my future. Please don't think because I think of him I don't want to be with you. My knee got a squeeze then and I knew he understood."

Chapter EIGHTEEN

This week was going to be one big roller coaster for me I was sure. It was now Monday and on Saturday afternoon at 4.45pm I was going to fly to New Zealand travelling on my own. That alone was a big step for me as I had never flown alone before, let alone on such a long journey. Still, as my mother had pointed out to me, I was flying first class which was fantastic and that it was going to be a wonderful adventure.

It was going to be a busy week as I had promised to go and see my gran in the nursing home and she had instructed me to "bring that lovely young man of yours with you," and had added "if only I was a few years younger....well quite a few" We had been invited to dinner at my brothers on the Wednesday and my mum too. My mum had also insisted that we do a 'ladies that lunch' on Tuesday, just her, me and Cassandra.

"She'll find somebody to have the boys I'm sure" mum had said. I wanted to get a present for Toby's parents although he had said it wasn't necessary I still wanted to get them something.

Mum, Cassie and I went into every shop in Guildford looking for something suitable but drew blank after blank until Cassie suddenly said "Why not just a picture of you guys on your wedding day but in a silver frame that is inscribed. Really boring I know but it is very personal and shows you have put some thought into it."

"Well it shows you put some thought into" I laughed but it is a great idea. So we found a nice frame and went off to lunch while they engraved it for me.

We had a wonderful evening on Wednesday with Mum, Cassie and Tom, and of course the boys, who won't let a visit from anybody go by without being totally involved, or for part of it anyway. Cassie cooked us a fantastic meal and after picking away on cheese for what seemed forever we drank glass after glass of port. It was a good job we were all staying over. I sat there and looked at my family, my beloved family, and thought just how very lucky I was.

The thought of the upcoming trial was in the back of our thoughts but none of us said a word about it, there was no way we were going to ruin this wonderful evening.

I was lucky that I didn't have to be called as a witness in the trial as I had already given so many statements and had video answered several questions from the defence lawyer. They had given me and Simon's other victims this choice because he intended to plead guilty. They said we had suffered enough and would not need to be in court where we would be looking at him. For this we were all grateful. I did wonder why he had so easily agreed to plead guilty, did he think it would be in his favour? I had no idea but was very glad anyway. They did say though that if there was any change in his plea we might be called, in which case Toby had said it could be adjourned until I could return from New Zealand, so I was going.....regardless of anything.

Friday night Toby took me for a curry. Not particularly romantic I know but as it is my favourite meal of all time he knew it would make me happy. We walked to the Indian and had a great meal with lots of wine. Then, in our drunken state, as soon as we got home, made fantastic love at least twice or maybe three times (Toby would say three anyway) that night.

Morning arrived all too soon and with rather heavy heads we showered and dragged ourselves down to the kitchen. Luckily I had had the forethought to pack the day before. If I had left it god know what I would have packed if I had left it to this morning!

Beside my coffee cup was a box, about the size of a packet of cigarettes, wrapped in beautiful gold wrapping paper and embellished with a huge gold bow. Toby was grinning at me.

"Go on then, open it" he said.

It was a beautiful gold charm bracelet. There were two charms on it, one was a heart about the size of the head of a drawing pin and the other, two tiny joined-together figurines, a bride and groom.

"Us" he said proudly "Forever."

I did cry then, not with sadness of going away from him but with so much love for him. He fixed the bracelet on my wrist and kissed my hand.

"Have a wonderful time darling, and I will be with you there very, very, soon, Oh and of course miss me."

My taxi arrived early afternoon leaving me plenty of time just in case of traffic and also so I could have a wander around the duty frees before my flight to maybe get some perfume etc.. I had decided to take a cab as I hate long drawn-out goodbyes and thought it would be easier. Anyway Toby was supposed to be at work really. We kissed a long lingering kiss at the door of the taxi, the driver was looking the other way for a bit but then turned and said "Aw common guys, I do have other fares to collect today" one more quick peck and I was in the cab and on my way to the airport.

As I was travelling first class I was treated like royalty. I was shown into this posh lounge where there was anything I wanted to drink and lots of stuff to eat. Not that I wanted to eat anything, but I don't know if I was because I was nervous or excited I did manage to sink three large gin and tonics before I boarded.

I was towards the front of the first class area and next to me was a lovely chatty American lady who told me her name was Nancy.

"First flight ?" she asked just as we were taking off. "It's just that I saw you holding on tightly to the arm rests as we took off! Don't worry sweetheart it's going to be a blast. I travel about twenty times a year, have done for donkeys years and nothing has ever happened to me yet!"

She was a bit of a life saver really as I was a little nervous. The flight attendants started the safety video which Nancy totally ignored of course, well, she said she flew twenty times a year so what did she have to learn about safety. She could probably tell them a thing or two. She prattled on and on but I was only half listening. Then the bit about switching off all phones and electrical devices etc came on and I remembered I hadn't turned off my phone. I took it out of my bag quickly and switched it off, thinking I would put in on flight safe mode and switch it back on later.

What I had no idea about at this moment was that there had been a collision back in London in the early hours of today involving a police prison transporter and a bus. Apparently (and totally unknown to me) the prison transporter was carrying three prisoners who were due to appear in court. One of them was Simon. One of the others was the boss of a massive drugs ring. The bus episode was obviously a fix. Three security guards had ended up in hospital. One had been killed and the three prisoners had escaped. Simon was free !!!!! and I had no idea.

I soon settled in my seat and put a movie on the small screen in front of me. It had been a while since I had been on a plane and then only on short flights to Spain and France. I had never seen the options available on the latest planes. Wow, I thought, I can watch movies that haven't even been released yet. I chose one featuring Brad

Pitt...what else...for two reasons. Firstly because it was a novelty and secondly Nancy would see I was engrossed in it and perhaps stop talking for a little while. She was a lovely woman but boy, could she talk. She had a real southern American accent which sounded nice for a short time but a little grating after a couple of hours.

As it was such a long journey there was going to be a stop off at Dubai for three hours. This turned out to be a real treat. Nancy, although still very chatty, was a perfect travelling companion after all. We went into the airport lounge and she both entertained and thrilled me with all her stories of her travels. She had a book publishing company and travelled all over the world meeting authors and outlets, book signings and lots and lots of parties. She had met so many people I suggested she write her autobiography. "That, my darling, will happen one day and when it does and you read it you had better hold on to your hat!"

The three hour stop over went in an instant with Nancy at the helm of our entertainment. And all too soon we were called back to continue our journey. I thanked Nancy for making my trip, so far anyway, so very memorable.

Chapter NINETEEN

Back on our flight I fiddled again to find another film to watch, but ended up watching the entire first series of Downton Abbey, one of my favourite TV dramas. Nancy was snoozing beside me making soft snoring noises which made me smile to myself.

A couple of hours into the second leg of our flight we were offered drinks and a little later more drinks and then a really nice dinner. I didn't know that they served such luxury on planes. We had proper cutlery and plates and everything. On the short flights I had experienced it was coffee in a paper cup or miniature spirit and tiny mixer can and a plastic glass hardly big enough for either. The TV series was good and then I tuned into a topical London magazine show. I was only half watching as I was beginning to feel a little drowsy until a ticker tape of current news began to appear across the bottom of the screen.

At first I thought I was seeing things but as I watched it again and again it began to dawn on me that it was current and true. It said there had been a crash in the city in the early hours of today and that three prisoners had escaped. Then it went on to name them. My drowsiness disappeared instantly as I watched in wonder at the tape.

Nancy leaned across and asked why I had suddenly started to whimper under my breath and to see just what was I looking at.

"Wow those are great dogs, do you have a dog at home?"

I realised she was actually watching the magazine program and they had six or seven types of huge long haired dogs. "I wouldn't want to have to groom one of them eh!" she said "I have a little Poodle myself, they don't moult you know. Oh I do miss him when I travel, still Bernie my husband looks after him while I'm away, he loves him almost as much as I do."

I had switched off from her conversation and I think she realised that, as she leaned back into her own seat and started fiddling with her monitor.

I was in shock, why hadn't Toby got in touch and told me what had happened, then I realised I hadn't switched my phone back on. Just at that moment the flight attendant asked I we wanted anything more to drink. The state I was in I would have drunk her bar dry, but I just asked for a bottle of wine.

Nancy gave me a strange look as if to say, what the hell, she then smiled a great big smile and she too asked for a bottle of wine. I have no idea just what the flight attendant thought but she obliged without comment, just a smile and a "certainly madam". I poured the first glass out and tried to get my head around what had happened. I was tempted to turn on my phone to see if I had received a text from Toby but I stopped short of doing it, deciding that I probably didn't really want to know what was going on in London. I'm sure they would catch him soon enough. That was a rubbish thought, he was incredible at disappearing.

A second glass of wine, then a third........

I feel like I'm floating, yes I am floating, up down, twisting like a kite. I am feeling like a feather, yes that's it, a beautiful white feather dancing in the breeze, I feel happy, content. More content than I have ever felt before, a strange feeling like I haven't a care in the whole wide world. Aarrrh floating, floating I feel free, I feel wonderful, I feel....what is that noise that has broken into my beautiful silent world, a loud noise, a harsh noise. I can't quite fathom what it is but it's getting louder and louder. I still have no idea but still it gets louder, louder, louder....it's screaming, I can hear screaming, I can hear so much screaming and shouting, I can hear people shouting then more screaming more screaming more screaming !!!!!

I am dead, I realise that now, and the screaming I heard was all the other people dying around me as the plane plummeted in to the ocean. I don't know quite how I feel other than very very sad. Sad that I will miss all the things I was hoping for in my new life. Arrrh my new life, I have waited for a long long time to get my new life and now it was ready to collect me I will miss it. The train that was to take me to my future has just left the station without me....no more looking forward, no more plans. I am dead !

"Tilly, Tilly", a gentle nudging suddenly is coming into my thoughts, what is going on, I am dead. Who is nudging me and how come I can feel it? I am dead...."Tilly Tilly are you alright" that voice again, that nudging. I am suddenly back in my seat in the plane. It is Nancy nudging me, she is leaning over me and her face is looking very concerned "Are you alright Tilly? You were screaming in your sleep, nearly woke all the other passengers up, did you have a bad dream dear?"

I'm not dead, I realise that now, it must all have been a terrible dream. My god I'm alive, I'm alive. I almost want to kiss Nancy with the relief of it.

"Too much wine deary" she is saying "you drank nearly a whole bottle, no wonder you had a bad dream."

The relief I feel is unbelievable. That dream was so real, but I'm alive.

"We'll be there soon" Nancy is saying. They'll be bringing us breakfast in an hour or so. Shall I call them and get them to bring you some coffee now?"

"No It's OK" I say. "I'll wait for the breakfast to come.

I am day dreaming, I really thought I was dead. Was it a dream? I turn to see Nancy with a mirror in one hand and a lipstick in the other. Surely if I am dead this wouldn't be happening.

"Nancy" I say and she turns to face me "Tell me I am not in a dream."

"You are definitely not in a dream" she is telling me "Was it a bad one then, that dream you just had?"

I don't know quite how to answer that as I am still not entirely sure this is real, was it a dream, it was so very vivid, am I alive or is this what it's like when you are dead?

"I know this is a funny question" I say "but can you tell me what day it is?"

Nancy is looking very puzzled "It's Sunday morning, remember we got on the plane on Saturday afternoon the fifteenth and now it is Sunday morning the sixteenth. Aah, sweetie! Are you getting a bit confused with the time differences?"

To say relief is washing over me is an understatement. So it was all a dream. I am alive, I am well, I am in a plane going to New Zealand to stay with my brand new in-laws and soon my darling new husband will be joining me.

"Are you feeling better now sweetheart" I hear Nancy saying "you are still very white."

"I'm fine now thank you" I say, "and do you know I am ready for some breakfast now - I'm starving!"

"Well I think it is on its way" she says "I can smell bacon."

Breakfast has arrived and I am tucking into mine as if I had never eaten before. After all, I have a life, I am alive and things are good. They have just cleared everything away and are now serving a second round of coffees.

"Shall we pop a little brandy in ours?" Nancy has just asked. Now I know it is early but what the hell,

"Yes why not" Nancy has just summoned an attendant to bring us a small brandy each.

"Here you are madam," I hear a voice that sounds a bit familiar, I am turning my head to say thank you, "Here you go MATILDA" !!!!!!!!...

BANG..

299

I feel like I'm floating, yes I am floating, up down, twisting like a kite. I am feeling like a feather, yes that's it, a beautiful white feather dancing in the breeze, I feel happy, content. More content than I have ever felt before, a strange feeling like I haven't a care in the whole wide world, arrrh floating, floating I feel free, I feel wonderful, I feel....what is that noise that has broken into my beautiful silent world, a loud noise, a harsh noise. I can't quite fathom what it is but it's getting louder and louder. I still have no idea but still it gets louder, louder, louder....it's screaming, I can hear screaming, I can hear so much screaming and shouting, I can hear people shouting then more screaming more screaming more screaming !!!!!

I am dead, I realise that now, and the screaming I heard was all the other people dying around me as the plane plummeted in to the ocean. I don't know quite how I feel other than very very sad. Sad that I will miss all the things I was hoping for in my new life. Arrrh my new life, I have waited for a long long time to get my new life and now it was ready to collect me I will miss it. The train that was to take me to my future has just left the station without me....no more looking forward, no more plans.

I am dead !

THE END

ABOUT THE AUTHOR

Jules lives in France with her husband and several horses, dogs, cats and ducks. They have been running a bed and breakfast for the past fourteen years but have now decided to retire in order to follow their passions of writing. Jules has been writing short stories for many years including several for her children when they were young.

She is very keen on cooking and baking and when she is not riding her horse or writing she indulges in such.

Printed in Great Britain
by Amazon